Nebraska Shoot-out

Jeff Arlen, a detective with the Butterworth Agency, is on the trail of Alec Frome, who has stolen $10000 from the bank where he works. Having lost him once, Arlen rides into Sunset Ridge, Nebraska, hoping to find Frome in the town where he'd once lived.

But after rescuing Brenda Farrell, soon after his arrival, he becomes side-tracked, drawn into a perilous local battle. Capturing Frome, and retrieving the stolen money looks like child's play in the face of what he now faces, which will only be resolved once and for all with tons of courage, and plenty of hot lead.

Nebraska Shoot-out

Corba Sunman

A Black Horse Western

ROBERT HALE · LONDON

© Corba Sunman 2014
First published in Great Britain 2014

ISBN 978-0-7198-1077-0

Robert Hale Limited
Clerkenwell House
Clerkenwell Green
London EC1R 0HT

www.halebooks.com

Typeset by
Derek Doyle & Associates, Shaw Heath
Printed and bound in Great Britain by
CPI Antony Rowe, Chippenham and Eastbourne

ONE

Jeff Arlen rode into the town of Sunset Ridge in Nebraska as evening drew in and shadows crawled across the wide main street. The sun was down beyond the high ridge that gave the town its name, and its heat waned as the solid rock of the ridge cut off its merciless rays. Arlen sighed with relief as he stepped down from his saddle in front of the stable and led his buckskin to the water trough by the main door. He had travelled far since dawn, and the long arduous miles had added discomfort upon discomfort to his ride.

Joe Henty, the stableman, old and garrulous, talked nonstop, and asked a string of questions as Arlen unsaddled his horse. Arlen, dressed in dusty range clothes, did not answer any personal questions. He was over six feet in height, broad-shouldered and lean. His handsome face was bronzed; brown eyes were filled with a harsh expression. He looked like a man who knew how to handle himself and should be avoided if possible. He wore a shell-belt around his waist, its loops filled with bright .45 cartridges; the holster low down on his right hip contained a .45 pistol that gleamed in the lamplight.

'Are you figuring on sticking around?' Henty asked, and paused for a reply. When one was not forthcoming he said: 'Mister, you look like a man who knows how many beans make five, but you wanta be careful in this burg. A lot of men have come to grief around here, and if you don't have business in town then you'll be wise to keep your head down and get to hell out before tomorrow's sunrise. That sure is good advice.'

'Thanks.' Arlen produced a silver dollar and flipped it in Henty's direction. It was deftly caught. 'That'll take care of my horse for the time I'll be in town. Give him a rub down and don't spare the oats. We've come a far piece in the past week. Is there a hotel?'

'Sure is.' Henty slid the dollar into a vest pocket. 'Slap bang in the middle of Main Street right opposite the law office. And here's another piece of good advice: steer clear of Sheriff Floren. He's hell on strangers, especially if they can't pay their way.'

'I've got no business with the law.' Arlen shrugged. 'They'll do well to keep out of my hair.'

'Say, that ain't the attitude to take.' Henty shook his head. 'You don't know about the set-up around here, because if you did you wouldn't talk like that. Whatever you do, don't run out of cash. Vagrancy is a law they enforce in this town with more effort than they put into hunting robbers.'

'I'll be long gone before the law knows I've been around.'

'It'll be your funeral.' Henty shook his head. 'I'll tell you this much, stranger. I have orders from the sheriff to report the arrival of every Johnny-come-lately who shows up, and I have to tell you to head for the law office before you do anything else.'

'Is that a fact?' A shadow of interest showed briefly on Arlen's face. 'What happens if you don't tell me?'

'I only tried it the once.' Henty turned away. 'I still got the bruises.'

Arlen walked to the door of the stable and glanced along the street. Lamps were shining in many windows, throwing small pools of radiance across the sidewalks. Figures were on the move around the street, flitting through the shadows, silent and anonymous. Arlen hitched up his gunbelt and headed for the saloon, which was advertising its presence with echoing piano music.

He took in his surroundings without appearing to do so. Long practice as a detective for the Butterworth Agency had sharpened his reflexes and welded in his mind the defensive attitude necessary for survival in his particular line of business. His present assignment was to locate Alec Frome, who had embezzled $10,000 from the United Cattleman's Bank, where he had worked in Dodge City, Kansas. On the face of it, Arlen thought he had a simple chore to perform – catch Frome and recover the money. But experience warned him not to take anything at face value.

He was anticipating trouble. He had followed Frome's trail from Dodge City but had lost it in west Kansas, and, by dint of using his experience in man hunting, he had arrived in Sunset Creek filled with hope that he would finally catch up with his quarry. But if he failed to locate the wanted man then his next step would be to retrace his steps to Kansas and take another look at where the trail had ended.

His first thought was to take care of his own needs, which meant eating, for nothing had passed his lips since before dawn. He went by the saloon without a sideways glance and paused outside a brightly illuminated establishment that seemed as popular as the saloon. A large sign over the doorway read: MIKE'S DINER. Arlen entered and slid into a seat at a table by the door. The place looked spotlessly clean. Three waitresses served the twenty or so tables, which were mainly occupied, and Arlen awaited his turn patiently.

The blonde waitress who came to take his order was dressed in pink – skirt and blouse – and wore a pink bow in her long brown hair. She smiled pleasantly. Arlen ordered beefsteak with all the trimmings and apple pie for a follow-up. He tried to relax as he awaited the arrival of the meal, but stiffened when the street door to his left was thrust open and a big man entered noisily The door slammed behind the newcomer with such force that every head in the place turned quickly at the sound. Arlen leaned back in his seat.

The man in the doorway was massively built, with wide, powerful shoulders. Everything about him was large. His hands were fleshy; his face round, almost featureless in spare flesh. His dark eyes were embedded in folds of creased flesh, his nose sprawled across his face above a traplike mouth, and his ears had thickened under the punishment of many fists over the years. He was wearing a brown town suit that was a size too small and had seen better days. A gunbelt was tight around his thick waist, and the holstered pistol was tied down on his right thigh. A silver deputy's badge glinted on the left lapel of his creased jacket. His expression was a permanent scowl.

Arlen took in the details of the newcomer, who was making a big show of studying the assembled diners, and he noted that most of the men present averted their gaze rather than meet the deputy's eyes. The big law man turned slowly, not missing a table in his inspection as he checked the room. His attitude showed innate aggression. His large face conveyed a sense of menace; his lower lip thrust forward, brown eyes almost disappearing in their nests of wrinkles as he frowned. His gaze finally reached Arlen and he thrust back his massive shoulders. A tight grin appeared on his thick lips as he dropped his right hand to the butt of his holstered gun.

'You're the stranger. I've been looking for you.' He spoke forcefully. 'Why ain't you reported to the sheriff?'

'I've got no business with the local law,' Arlen replied.

'Didn't Henty tell you to go straight to the law office?'

'I'm not in the habit of taking orders from a stable-man.'

'Is that so? I'm Elk Mitchell, the number two lawman in this burg, and I'm telling you now to head for the law office.'

Arlen saw the waitress bringing his meal, but she paused at the sight of Mitchell, and when she hesitated Arlen called to her.

'If that's my food, miss, then bring it over.'

'Maybe you don't hear so good,' Mitchell rasped.

'All I hear is a blowhard trying to cause a public nuisance,' Arlen responded. 'I'll see the sheriff after I've eaten. Now get out of here and leave me in peace. I ain't ever suffered from indigestion, and I don't intend to start now, so get lost.'

Mitchell reached for his gun, but halted the movement when he found himself staring at the muzzle of Arlen's pistol. He blinked in shock, because he had never seen a faster draw. His mouth gaped and his eyes opened wide.

'So you've got a one-track mind,' Arlen said. 'OK, take out your gun and throw it on the floor under my table.' He waited until Mitchell had obeyed. 'Now sit down at the table behind you with your back to me and place your hands on the top of your head. You better not do more than blink your eyes until I tell you to get up. After I've eaten we'll see the sheriff. While I'm eating, you keep still and bite your lip.'

Mitchell looked as if he would disobey, but the threat of Arlen's steady pistol persuaded him that it would be good sense to comply. He dropped heavily into a vacant chair at the next table and did not move a muscle while Arlen enjoyed his meal. When he had finished, Arlen paid the waitress and picked up Mitchell's gun. He unloaded the weapon and threw it on the table in front of the deputy.

'Let's go,' he said.

Mitchell sprang to his feet, snatched up his gun and stuffed it into his holster. He turned to the door, and preceded Arlen across the darkened street to the law office. Arlen stayed back out of reach and kept his right hand close to the butt of his holstered gun. Mitchell kicked open the door of the law office and strode inside. Arlen followed and closed the door.

The sheriff was seated at his desk in a corner of the big office, working on some papers. He looked up quickly at the interruption, and grinned when he saw Arlen and his deputy. Arlen took an immediate dislike to the chief lawman. The sheriff was tall and thin, his cheeks sunken, his blue eyes set well back under his lined forehead. His nose was long, his mouth small with thin lips that were pinched as if he was full of vinegar.

'So you got him,' the sheriff said. 'He doesn't look like he gave you any trouble.'

'You've got hold of the wrong end of the stick, Sheriff,' Arlen said.

Mitchell opened his mouth as if to speak. Arlen looked at him and cut in.

'Your deputy started something he couldn't finish. I brought him here – he didn't bring me.'

The sheriff's face changed expression. He pushed back his chair and got to his feet, his right hand dropping to the butt of his holstered gun. Arlen regarded him without expression and waited stoically.

'I'm Gus Floren, the county sheriff.' A smile stretched the thin lips. 'We often get troublemakers coming into town, which is why I make a point of seeing every stranger before he has the chance to cut loose.' He paused and his smile widened. 'And we know how to handle tough guys. What's your name?'

'I'm Jeff Arlen, a detective with the Butterworth Detective Agency, head office in Chicago, and I'm hunting a man called Alec Frome, a bank cashier who embezzled ten thousand dollars from the United Cattleman's Bank in Dodge City.'

'Is Frome here in town?' Floren demanded.

'I don't know.' Arlen shrugged. 'I lost his trail between

11

here and the Kansas line.'

'What does he look like? If he's in my bailiwick then I'll help you find him.'

'I don't need help, or interference.' Arlen had seen a gleam come into Floren's eyes at the mention of the stolen money. He glanced at the motionless Elk Mitchell and saw a wolfish expression on the big deputy's face. Arlen remained expressionless as a warning sounded in his mind, but he felt as if he had walked into an ambush, and readied himself for trouble.

'I run the law in this county according to the needs of the people,' Floren said. 'We get a lot of human trash flocking up here from Kansas, and we're mighty strict with them. They would overrun us if we didn't hit them hard. The man you're looking for comes into that category, and it's our sworn duty to spare no effort to catch him. I'll give you a free hand to do your own investigation, but we will make enquiries and do what we can to help you get your man. So we'd better work together on this. You'll soon have your felon under arrest to take back to Dodge City.'

'That's OK by me, Sheriff,' Arlen replied. 'Frome is in his late forties, small and wiry. He's running to fat – easy living, I guess, and he dresses well in a good suit. He looks like a dude from back East – wears a diamond stick-pin in his cravat. He worked in the bank in Dodge for twenty years before he disappeared with the missing dough. And he's pretty good at concealing his tracks. This is not the first time I've lost him, but I reckon to catch him before long.'

'Before he can spend that stolen dough,' observed Mitchell, and laughed hoarsely.

'I reckon Frome came from these parts before he went to work in the Dodge bank,' Arlen continued. 'I questioned the bank staff, and one of them reported that he'd heard Frome talking about Sunset Ridge and Clinton County in Nebraska. His tracks have led me in this direction, so I think that information is correct.'

'I never heard the name Frome around here.' Floren shook his head. 'But I'll make enquiries in the town. I'll likely get more assistance from the locals than you will, seeing you're a stranger.'

'Thanks.' Arlen prepared to leave. 'Bear in mind that Frome may be an assumed name. But I reckon I'll have to backtrack to Aspen Creek in Kansas. That's the last place I got positive proof that he was heading this way.'

'We'll give it our best shot.' Floren smiled. 'You can count on my cooperation, Arlen. I'll pull out all the stops on this. Keep me informed of your actions and let me know if you have any luck in running down the fugitive.'

Arlen nodded and departed, filled with doubt about Floren and Mitchell. He went back across the street to the hotel and rented a room, then returned to the livery barn to collect his gear. After putting his saddle-bags and rifle in his hotel room he left to look around the town, then he turned his steps towards the saloon. As he passed a vacant lot where a new building was being erected he heard a woman's voice coming from the dense shadows and paused to look around. The night sky was pale with reflected moonlight. The noise of loud music emanating from the nearby saloon was blotting out most of the natural noises of the night. Arlen wondered if he had imagined the sound, but it had been a woman's voice, and

13

filled with fear.

The sound came again – a female voice raised in distress. The sound echoed from the darkness. Arlen looked round to pinpoint the sound, then set off swiftly across the vacant lot. He paused after some yards and again listened intently, then went forward when he heard the ominous sounds of altercation. He rounded a stack of lumber and almost walked into three figures in the dense shadows. One was a woman with a man holding her by the arms from behind while a second man confronted her. Moonlight glinted on the long blade of a skinning knife that was being held dangerously close to the woman's throat by the second man.

Arlen's approach had been silent. The two men were intent on their captive. The man with the knife had his back to Arlen. He was asking the woman a question. She struggled to free herself from the second man's clutches as she shook her head violently. Arlen drew his pistol, grabbed the man's knife arm in a vicelike grip, and slammed the long barrel of his gun against the man's forehead.

The man dropped instantly. The second man recovered from his shock, thrust the woman at Arlen, and turned to run. Arlen shot him in the right leg. The crash of the shot echoed loudly. The woman thudded against Arlen, who braced himself and steadied her. He released her to check on the two men. He picked up the discarded knife, then found that its owner was unconscious with a bloodied face. He removed a pistol from the man's belt, and then went to the second man, who was lying on the ground, clutching his right thigh with both hands. Arlen took a gun from the man's holster and turned to confront the woman. She was leaning against the stacked timber with her head down, resting on an outstretched arm.

'What was going on here?' Arlen demanded.

The woman raised her head. Moonlight shone full on her pale, taut face. She was young, no more than twenty, he reckoned, and despite her shock she looked attractive. She was breathing deeply, and Arlen placed a hand fleetingly on her shoulder.

'It's OK now,' he said reassuringly. 'The danger is over. Those two won't bother you again. What did they want with you?'

'Money,' she replied tonelessly. 'They confronted me on the sidewalk and brought me over here. When one of them produced the knife I thought I should die.'

'What were you doing out alone after dark?'

'I don't live in town. I came in from our ranch to see my friend Jane, and left it a bit late to return home. Jane wanted me to stay the night but I knew my father would worry if I didn't go home because I hadn't made arrangements to stay in town.'

Arlen glanced around and saw two figures on the sidewalk. He recognized Elk Mitchell's big figure and called loudly to attract attention. Both men came across the lot, and were holding their pistols when they confronted Arlen. Sheriff Floren was with Mitchell.

'Did you fire that shot?' Floren demanded, recognizing Arlen.

Arlen explained the incident as he had seen it. When he mentioned the two men, Mitchell went around the timber stack, and came back, dragging the men with him.

'Who are they, Elk?' Floren demanded.

''Strangers,' Mitchell replied. 'I'll throw them in a cell until you can get around to them. I'll ask them some questions.'

'Did they demand money, Miss Farrell?' Floren asked the girl.

'Yes, Sheriff.' She explained the incident in a tremulous tone.

Arlen moved impatiently, but his mind was busy. He was wondering how two strangers could be in town without the local law knowing of their presence. He watched Sheriff Floren's indistinct features as the lawman continued to ask questions of the shocked girl, and sensed that his attitude to the situation was fraudulent. Floren, with his keen watch on newcomers, should know of the presence of two strangers in town.

'You'd better come along to the law office and make a statement about this,' Floren said at length.

'I can't do that, Sheriff,' she protested, her tone rising. 'I have to get home before my father sends out a search party for me. I'll come into town tomorrow and see you.'

'You shouldn't be riding home alone after dark,' Floren said. 'I'll send Elk along with you.'

'I'd rather ride alone!' She stifled a shudder, and Arlen saw distaste in her expression.

'You won't ride alone, miss,' he said quietly. 'I'll see you home.'

Arlen didn't quite know why he made the offer. It was none of his business, and he had his own job to consider. But there was a nagging sensation in the back of his mind. The local law had dropped on to him within minutes of

16

his failure to report to them after the stableman had informed them of his presence in town, and he could not accept that two apparent criminals had been overlooked. He did not believe the men were strangers to the sheriff, and sensed that Elk Miller had lied when he said they were. So he reckoned there was a mystery here that needed looking into.

The girl did not protest at Arlen's decision, and the sheriff nodded.

'That's OK by me,' Floren said easily. 'I'll see you sometime tomorrow. Give my regards to Buck when you get home. Look me up in the morning, Arlen.'

'I'll do that,' Arlen promised.

Floren departed. The girl took a step towards the sidewalk, and almost lost her balance. Arlen grasped her elbow, and could feel that she was shaking. She was breathing noisily, and he suspected that she was badly shocked.

'Steady on,' he advised. 'You've had a bad fright. But it's over now. Did you ride into town?'

'My horse is in the stable,' she replied, leaning on his supporting hand.

'And so is mine. We'll collect them together. Where do you live, Miss Farrell?'

'About five miles south of here, on the Bar F ranch. You don't have to see me home, Mr Arlen.'

'My friends call me Jeff,' he replied. 'And I do have to see you home. You need company after the shock you've received, and having rescued you from a nasty situation, I insist on seeing you safely to your door. I know I'm a stranger to you, but I'm sure, after what has happened, that you'll regard me as a friend.'

'Thank you, Jeff. I'm so grateful that you came along when you did.' They walked on together, heading for the livery barn. 'Have you been in town long?'

'I arrived about an hour ago,' he responded, his features hardening as he considered. 'Did you get a look at the faces of those two men?'

'I'll never forget the one who held the knife at my throat,' she replied, and a tremor passed through her.

'If you feel up to it perhaps you'll tell me exactly happened and what was said,' he suggested.

'I was on my way to the stable when they confronted me,' she said hesitantly. 'They grasped my arms and walked me on to the vacant lot. Only one of them did the talking. He warned me not to make a sound, and then asked for money. When I said I had no more than a dollar or two he took out the knife and held it against my throat. I thought my last minute had come. But then he began talking about someone I didn't know. He told me to give a message to my father. I didn't have any idea what he was talking about, and when I protested he told me to give the warning to my father, that I didn't need to know anything more.'

'What is the message you were told to give your father?'

'I have to tell him to go to Room Nine at the hotel on Saturday evening. A man called Rufus Sandor will be waiting for him.'

'So their demand for money was not the real reason they held you up.'

'I think they would have robbed me if you had not come along.'

They reached the stable and were accosted by Joe

18

Henty. The stableman emerged from his dusty office, holding a lantern shoulder high in order to get a good look at them.

'I didn't think you'd be going home tonight, Brenda,' he declared. 'I saw your horse in its stall about an hour gone, and reckoned you was staying overnight.' He looked Arlen up and down. 'Did you report to the sheriff like I told you?'

'I've seen him,' Arlen said. 'How many strangers have come into town in the last two days?'

'You're the only one, so far as I know.' Henty shrugged. 'I only see the ones who put their nags in here. I wouldn't know about anyone else.'

Arlen was thoughtful as he saddled his horse. When the girl led her mount out of the stall he was waiting for her just inside the big street door. They led their animals outside and mounted. Arlen looked around as they rode off at a canter, and when he spotted a figure detaching itself from a corner of the big barn he kicked his feet clear of his stirrups and dived sideways out of the saddle.

A gun crashed and red muzzle flame speared through the shadows. Arlen left his saddle, and as he fell against the girl beside him he heard the ominous crackle of a closely passing bullet.

TWO

Arlen grasped the girl with his left hand and steadied her as he sprawled almost across her saddle. He snatched at his reins with his right hand as his feet hit the ground. The horses were moving at a canter and he lost his balance and fell. He twisted on to his left side as the horses went on, and drew his pistol. He looked towards the corner of the barn and saw a figure moving in the shadows. The ambusher's gun fired again and Arlen closed his eyes to avoid being dazzled by the muzzle flame. He cocked his pistol, opened his eyes, and fired two shots at the spot where the gun flash had originated.

Brenda returned with his horse as he regained his feet. He probed the shadows over by the barn, but now there was no sign of his attacker. He holstered his gun and mounted his horse. The girl's face was just a pale oval in the moonlight, and he looked at her intently.

'Are you OK?' he asked. 'I'm sorry I was a bit rough when I left my saddle, but there was no time to warn you. I spotted a figure in the shadows and guessed what was coming.'

'I think there's trouble coming to this county,' she replied.

'What makes you think that? Is it because those two men attacked you?'

She rode on without replying, and Arlen spurred his horse to regain her side.

'Tell me about the trouble,' he said.

'I wouldn't know where to begin. The sheriff makes a big show of keeping undesirables out of town, but there are some strangers around who are not bothered by him.'

'Do you think he's failing in his job?' Arlen glanced around alertly. They drew away from the town and followed the trail south, which showed up plainly in the moonlight.

'It's not for me to say.' She shrugged. 'What line of business are you in?'

'I'm a detective working for Phil Butterworth, who learned his business with Allan Pinkerton and his outfit in Chicago in the early days. Butterworth eventually branched out on his own and I've been kept busy ever since I joined him three years ago. It's a hard life, but quite rewarding.'

'Are you on a case right now?'

'I am, but I can't talk about it.'

'You're mighty handy with your gun. I was wondering if you could handle a strong-arm job for my father?'

'So he's got trouble. Can you talk about it?'

'I'd rather leave it to Dad to tell you, if you're interested in a job. I don't know much about it, you understand. All I've seen are things happening around the ranch. The trouble is, everything fades into the background for a spell, then comes back into the open like a prairie fire, and seems to get worse each time it reappears. Just lately, Dad has been hinting at hiring a gunhand.'

'And that message you got from the two men earlier had something to do with your father's trouble, huh?'

'That's how it seems. I don't think they really meant to rob me. It was their way of passing on a message.'

'Who is Rufus Sandor?'

'I don't know. I'd never heard of him before tonight.'

Arlen fell silent and they continued. He eventually sighted a cluster of ranch buildings ahead, and a little later they rode into a yard. A dog barked as they made for the porch of the house, where lamplight spilled across the yard from a front window. A man moved forward out of the shadows, and Arlen saw a rifle in his hands.

'You're late, Brenda,' the man said. 'You know I like you back home before the shadows thicken. Sunset Creek ain't the place at night for a young woman on her own. I wish you would think of the dangers and not be so casual about yourself.'

'I'm sorry, Dad. I got held up as I was leaving town.' Brenda slid out of her saddle. 'This is Jeff Arlen. He kindly escorted me home. Jeff, this is my father, Buck Farrell.'

'Howdy, Mr Farrell.'

'Howdy, Arlen. It was good of you to see Brenda home. Get down and come into the house.'

As Arlen dismounted a man appeared from the dense shadows around the end of the porch. He was holding a long gun ready for use.

'Is everything OK, boss?' he demanded.

'Fine, Jake,' Farrell replied. 'Brenda has come home.

Take care of her horse, will you? I need to talk to her.'

'OK.' Jake came forward and took up the reins of Brenda's horse. He was a tall man, lean but solid. He looked at Arlen questioningly.

'Jeff Arlen, meet Jake Pearson,' Brenda introduced.

They acknowledged each other and Pearson led the girl's horse away. Buck Farrell entered the house and Arlen followed Brenda inside. He looked intently around the big living room, liking what he saw. It was essentially a man's room, but there were feminine touches, like the vase of flowers in the centre of the long table and the flowered material of the drapes at the windows.

Farrell was short and well-fleshed. His sparse hair was turning grey to match the colour of his pale eyes. He was in his early fifties, and his expression showed that he was a worried man.

'Sit down,' Farrell invited. Arlen pulled out a chair at a corner of the table and dropped into it. 'I smell trouble on you,' Farrell continued, looking at Brenda. 'What happened?'

Arlen listened intently to the girl's account on the incident, and watched Farrell's face for reaction. Farrell stiffened at the mention of Rufus Sandor, but said nothing.

'Who is Sandor, Dad?' Brenda asked. 'You've never mentioned him. Is he a friend from way back?'

'He was never a friend to any man,' Farrell said heavily. 'So he's showed up at last.' He shrugged. 'All I can say is that it took him a lot longer than I thought it would.'

Arlen considered what was being said, but could glean nothing from the bare facts, although he had become aware of the raw fear that seemed to be stacking up in the big room. Brenda was badly worried, and her experience in town had robbed her of confidence. She was watching her father's face intently, and evidently coming to the same conclusion as Arlen.

'If Sandor was never a friend then he must have been an enemy,' she probed.

'Don't worry your head about him. I'll see him in town like he suggests, and settle the dust between us.'

'That sounds like gun trouble unless I'm very much mistaken.' Brenda glanced fleetingly at Arlen, then drew a deep breath. 'Jeff told me he is a detective with Butterworth's agency. Perhaps he can help you, Dad.'

'I don't need any help.' A note of finality sounded in Farrell's tone and Arlen knew no amount of talking by his daughter would shift his attitude. But Farrell looked at him searchingly. 'So you're a detective, huh?' He nodded to himself. 'It seems too much of a coincidence that a range detective should turn up here just when I'm getting trouble. Does your job have anything to do with me, Arlen?'

'No, it's a coincidence. I'm on a case that led me into this area, and I happened to be on hand to help Brenda. That's all there is to my presence here, and I'd better be getting back to town now to follow my own line of enquiry.'

'I'm mighty grateful to you for helping Brenda.' Farrell sighed heavily. 'Don't think I'm not. I have no idea what's going on in town, but I advise you to watch your step.'

'I'll surely do that.'

'Take care on your return to town,' Farrell continued.

24

'We're bothered by nightriders on this range, and they might mistake you for somebody else.'

'I'm always careful,' Arlen replied with a tight smile. 'Goodnight.'

He turned to the door and Brenda accompanied him out to the porch. She reached out and grasped his left wrist.

'Don't be put off by Dad's manner, Jeff,' she begged. 'I can tell he's badly worried. Normally he would have made a big thing of the way you took care of me.'

'But he's not prepared to talk about his trouble,' Arlen replied. 'And I can't stick my nose into a man's business unless he asks for help.'

'Can I hire you to do some checking up?' she asked.

'I work for an agency. You'd have to go through my office in Dodge, but I think they would turn you down because I'm on a big case right now.'

He heard her sigh, and felt sympathy for her. 'I'll tell you what I'll do,' he said quietly. 'I'm a sucker for a pretty face, and I don't like the way those two hardcases handled you. I must make preliminary inquiries around town about the man I'm after, and if I can get some time to myself I'll take a look around and try to see which way the wind is blowing.'

'I'd be grateful if you would do that. I don't care what it'll cost. I'm afraid for Dad's life. I have no idea what happened in his past, but the men involved seem to be bad.'

'I'll know by noon tomorrow if my man is anywhere around,' Arlen told her. 'If I don't find signs of him then I'll have to backtrack some. I'll head out the day after tomorrow, but I can give you the rest of tomorrow. Can you meet me in town around noon?'

'I'll be there if I have to ride through hell and high water,' she replied.

'I'll be at the hotel,' Arlen said. He spun round when he heard the sound of a boot scraping on the porch, and relaxed when Jake Pearson stepped into view.

'Brenda, I heard riders out on the range,' Pearson reported. 'Tell Buck, will you? I'm going out to take a look around.'

Pearson turned on his heel and hurried back into the shadows. A moment later the sound of receding hoofs echoed across the yard.

'I must tell Dad,' Brenda said.

'So I'll see you at the hotel in town at noon tomorrow,' Arlen called as she said goodbye and went into the house.

Arlen untied his horse from the porch rail and swung into the saddle. He crossed the yard, and paused on the trail to town, his thoughts moving swiftly. He was intrigued by the apparent mystery surrounding Buck Farrell, and on a whim he turned his horse away from town and rode in the direction Pearson had taken. When he paused on the edge of the ranch he heard the dull thudding of hoofs in the distance, and shook his head ruefully as he set out to follow. What he was doing was against all the rules of his tough business, but an image of Brenda Farrell's face was emblazoned on the screen of his mind and he could only follow the dictates of his nature.

He picked up the sound of a horse crossing a stretch of hard ground and went on carefully in the same direction, hoping that Pearson was concentrating on the riders ahead and was not watching his back trail. Moonlight silvered the range, and Arlen had to remain well in the rear to avoid being seen. He was experienced in tracking and trailing, and followed Pearson unerringly through the shadows, carefully avoiding bright patches of moonlight.

An hour passed. Arlen reckoned the riders were rustlers, and was prepared to step into the situation on Pearson's side if shooting broke out. But eventually the squat shape of a line shack showed ahead, with four horses standing outside it. Arlen was surprised when Pearson rode in openly, and he turned aside into a small stand of timber to dismount. He could hear the sound of moving water near by, but did not see the stream responsible for it. He went forward on foot, keeping to the shadows, and managed to get close to the shack. He saw Pearson's horse tethered with the other four, and wondered about the situation.

He gained the rear of the shack and pressed close to the sun-warped boards. The mumble of voices came from within but he could not hear what was being said. But he did not need to ask if Pearson knew these strangers, for the man had ridden right in and joined them. What he wanted to know was what Pearson's business was. He did not think the man was acting in the interests of his boss.

Minutes passed, then the voices sounded louder: Pearson emerged from the shack and the strangers accompanied him.

'OK,' Pearson said. 'I'd better get back. Tell Sandor that Farrell will be in town to see him as arranged, and Sandor had better watch out for the man who brought Brenda Farrell home this evening. His name is Arlen, and he's a detective.'

There was laughter from the four men. Pearson's voice faded as he rode away from the shack. The four strangers mounted and rode off in a different direction. Arlen stood motionless in the heavy silence while his thoughts roved over what he had heard. Then he went back to his horse, and, as he swung into the saddle, Pearson's voice came to him.

'Get your hands up. I got you covered so don't try anything. So you followed me from the ranch, huh? That was real smart of you, but not too clever. Your horse gave you away. I'm gonna have to kill you, mister.'

'What's your business, Pearson?' asked Arlen as he raised his hands shoulder high. 'It looks to me like you're biting the hand that feeds you. Who were those riders you met, and who is Rufus Sandor?'

'I guessed you'd spell trouble the minute I laid eyes on you,' Pearson responded. 'That's why I eavesdropped when Brenda took you into the house.'

'Answer my questions,' Arlen rapped.

'You won't need the answers where you're going. Turn around and I'll take your gun. If you know any prayers you better start saying them.'

Arlen turned, and heard Pearson's feet as the man approached him. Arlen glanced over his shoulder and saw that Pearson was holding his pistol in his right hand. He looked to his front again, and when the muzzle of the gun jabbed against his spine he spun around instantly, dropping his hands as he did so. His left arm went down over Pearson's gun arm and he pinioned it against his body. Pearson fired a shot, but his muzzle was no longer aligned with Arlen's body and the bullet thudded into a tree trunk.

Completing his movement, Arlen grabbed at Pearson's gun hand, his fingers closing around the hand and trapping the index finger inside the trigger guard. He jerked his hand sharply to the right, heard the bone in Person's finger snap, and pulled the gun out of Pearson's grasp. He stepped back, swung the gun, and slammed the long barrel against Pearson's left temple. Pearson fell instantly and lay motionless.

Arlen heaved a sigh as he bent and searched the man, relieving him of a knife that was in a sheath on the back of the gunbelt. Pearson groaned and stirred. Arlen waited patiently for him to recover. When Pearson eventually sat up, Arlen spoke sharply.

'You'd better come up with some good answers to the questions bothering me, Pearson. We'll take them one at a time. Who is Rufus Sandor?'

'I've never heard of him,' Pearson rasped.

'You mentioned his name to those four men,' Arlen reminded him, 'so spill the beans.'

'You're barking up the wrong tree.' Pearson shook his head. 'I ain't telling you a damn thing, so what are you gonna do?'

'I'll take you back to the ranch and throw the whole situation into Farrell's lap.'

Under the threat of Arlen's ready gun, Pearson led the way to where he had left his horse. They swung in their saddles and, Pearson in front, they rode back to the Bar F ranch. As they crossed the yard, Buck Farrell's voice called a challenge to them. Arlen replied quickly. Farrell stepped forward on the porch with a Winchester in his hands.

'I thought you'd gone back to town, Arlen,' the rancher

said. 'What's going on?'

'I'll tell you when we get inside the house,' Arlen replied. He kept Pearson covered with the pistol when they dismounted, and urged him on to the porch.

Farrell opened the door and stepped aside. Pearson entered the house and Arlen followed closely, his gun levelled at the hapless cowboy. Brenda Farrell jumped up from a big leather chair and put down a book she had been reading. Her smile of welcome at the sight of Arlen faded when she saw the gun in his hand.

'What's happening?' she demanded.

Farrell closed the door. The butt of his rifle was tucked into his right armpit. He looked at Pearson's set face and then turned his attention to Arlen.

'It's a good thing I didn't ride back to town,' Arlen said. 'I reckoned Pearson might have needed help against those mystery riders so I tailed him.' He went on to explain the incident at the line shack, then fell silent.

Farrell gazed fixedly at Pearson, and the muzzle of his rifle lifted until it was pointing at the cowboy's chest.

'So you're a snake in the grass.' Farrell spoke as if the words were burning his lips. 'You're running with Sandor. I guess that explains a lot that's been going on around here. I've had suspicions about you, Pearson, so what kind of a hold has the Sandor got on you? He ruined my family years ago, and he sure knows how to get a grip on a man's throat.'

Pearson did not reply. He gazed defiantly at Farrell. Arlen watched them intently, wondering what was going on. Brenda came forward and confronted Pearson. Anger sparkled in her dark eyes. She shook her head slowly in disbelief, and then heaved a sigh and stepped back as if Pearson would contaminate her.

'My dad took you in and gave you a good job, Jake,' she said quietly. 'And this is how you repay his kindness. Have you stabbed him in the back?'

'I did what I had to,' Pearson said.

'You could have warned Dad about what was happening instead of going along with Sandor's business, whatever it is.' She turned to Farrell, and the tone of her voice changed. 'It's time you told me what is going on, Dad,' she said firmly. 'And don't say it's none of my business! It's getting a little too late in the day for you to cover up. Who is Sandor, and what is he after? How can he affect your life like this? Why should he put Pearson in here to spy on you, or whatever it was he was doing?'

'It's my business,' Farrell said brusquely, 'and I'll handle it my way. I've done nothing wrong, if that's what you're thinking, so don't get worked up about it.' He looked into Pearson's eyes. 'Get off my ranch but fast, and don't show your face around here again or I'll shoot you. Get moving. You've got five minutes to shake the dust off.'

Pearson departed hurriedly. Arlen holstered his gun and prepared to leave, but paused on his way to the door and turned to Farrell.

'Maybe I'd better stick around until Pearson has gone?' he suggested.

'Thanks but there's no need. I can handle Pearson. Thanks for what you did. I'm doubly beholden to you.'

'I'm glad I was able to help.' Arlen caught Brenda's eye and nodded. She blinked her eyelids in tacit acknowledgement and he left the house.

31

He stood for some moments in the shadows on the porch, just looking around the silent yard. Pearson emerged from the bunkhouse and entered the corral. Arlen stood motionless until the cowboy had saddled up and was ready to leave. When Pearson rode out to the south, Arlen went in the opposite direction towards town. He remained alert, his eyes strained to pierce the night. It was a little darker now, for the moon had disappeared behind a ridge of cloud. His mind was active as he considered his experiences since reaching Sunset Ridge earlier.

The lights of the town were a welcome sight. He rode into the main street and dismounted outside the stable. Joe Henty appeared in the big doorway of the barn and held out his hand for the reins of the horse as Arlen led the animal into the doorway.

'I'll put him away for you,' Henty said. 'I liked what you did for Brenda Farrell earlier.'

'It was my pleasure,' Arlen responded. He said nothing about subsequent events out at the Farrell ranch and turned to leave.

'Elk Mitchell was snooping around after you pulled out with Brenda,' Henty said. 'He asked me what you talked about when you first rode in. You wanta watch out for the local law because you could find all kinds of trouble if they take an interest in you. They run a chain gang in this county, and you'll get a six-month sentence to work on it for any reason they can think up. Don't say I haven't warned you.'

'I don't think they'll bother me,' Arlen said easily. 'Did you hear the shooting when I rode out with Brenda?'

Henty nodded. 'I heard it but didn't take any notice. It

ain't wise to stick your nose in anything around here.'

'Did you see anyone acting suspiciously around the barn at the time?'

'I know better than to look outside when guns are popping.'

Arlen took his leave. He went to the hotel and, finding the lobby deserted, went behind the reception desk to glance through the hotel register, although he didn't expect Frome to use his real name. There were several recent entries, and he pressed his hand on the top of the small bell standing on the desk. A moment later a door in the back wall opened and a man emerged from the office.

'I'm interested in anyone who booked into the hotel during the last couple of days,' Arlen said.

'I can't give out details of hotel guests,' the man replied.

Arlen reached into a pocket and produced his identification. The man studied it and then shook his head.

'I give the local law details of everyone who stays here,' he said. 'There's no reason why you can't ask them for help. They are not bound by the rules I abide by. It's more than my job is worth to divulge information about hotel guests.'

'Let's put it this way,' said Arlen. 'The man I'm looking for is a snappy dresser.' He described Frome, and the clerk shook his head before Arlen could finish.

'I never saw anyone who looked like that,' he asserted.

'I could have you arrested for withholding information,' Arlen said sharply. 'Apart from being a private detective, I am also sworn in as a special deputy US marshal. So you better start cooperating or you could find yourself working on the local chain gang.'

'There was a man looking like the person you described in here four days ago. He stayed one night, and said he was going to Colorado – Denver to be precise.'

'That's better.' Arlen nodded. 'Did he have much luggage?'

'A couple of bags, that's all. One he put in the hotel safe overnight.'

'Did he report his presence to the local law?'

'I wouldn't know anything about his doings outside the hotel.'

Arlen turned away. He left the hotel and walked to the saloon. There were some thirty men at the long bar. Arlen entered and stood to the right of the batwings, looking around. There were a number of small tables dotted around the floor space, some being used by drinkers and others with poker players concentrating on their cards. The bar was fully attended, and three bartenders were hard at work, serving thirsty customers. A fourth man was standing behind the bar just watching the business. He was tall and lean, dressed in a black suit, white shirt, and had a black string tie around his neck. The chain of a pocket watch, stretched across his stomach, glinting in the lamplight. He was glancing around with a gaze that missed nothing, and when he looked in Arlen's direction he stiffened and watched him intently.

Arlen went to the near corner of the bar and the smartly dressed man came to him, a smile stretching his thin lips.

'I'm Tom Frazee,' he said in a smooth tone. 'I own this place. What'll it be?'

'Three fingers of rye and a beer chaser,' Arlen replied.

Frazee turned away and returned a few moments later with a whiskey and a beer. He looked into Arlen's eyes and said:

'You're a detective from Chicago. I saw you in action there two years ago. You picked up a bank robber. I never forget a face. So what are you doing in this neck of the woods?'

'I'm looking for a man.' Arlen tossed a silver coin on to the bar top.

Frazee pushed the coin back to him. 'I couldn't take your money after I saw what you did to that bank robber. It's a privilege to buy you a drink.'

'Thanks.' Arlen picked up his dollar and pocketed it. He drank half his whiskey and put the glass back on the bar. 'You get all kinds in here, I guess.' He described Frome and Frazee shook his head.

'I'd remember him if I saw him,' he said. 'What did he do?'

'I can't divulge details, but he would have plenty of money on him. He's a real classy dresser.'

'Then I wish I had seen him.' Frazee smiled as if he had made a joke, and Arlen glimpsed the glint of gold in his mouth. 'I'll keep an eye open for him, and let you know if I see him.'

'Thanks.' Arlen finished his whiskey and then drank his beer. 'I'm for an early night,' he commented, and departed.

He stood in the shadows on the sidewalk and let his thoughts have free rein while his hard gaze checked out his surroundings. He had his job to do, and could not afford to be sidetracked by local trouble. But he had an image of Brenda Farrell's face on the screen of his mind and knew he would break the rules of his business by trying to help her. He could not walk away and leave her to whatever trouble was closing in around her father.

He hitched up his gunbelt and moved on, intending to visit the law office to find out more about the two men who had accosted Brenda Farrell. He stepped down off the sidewalk and started across the street, but had barely covered three yards when two guns began shooting at him from the darkness opposite. Muzzle flames spurted and he threw himself full length in the dust, his gun coming to hand with practised ease. The silence was broken by the hammering reports of the weapons, and bullets crackled around him. He raised his gun and began to return fire.

THREE

Arlen triggered his pistol, throwing lead at the gun flashes. He was surprised by the attack, and wondered remotely who was after his blood. He flattened out when his gun was empty and grabbed fresh shells from his cartridge belt. By the time he was ready to resume the action the shooting had ceased and echoes were grumbling away across the town. Several dogs were barking furiously as he got to his feet. He ran across the street, pinpointing the spot where he had seen the gun flashes, and pulled up short in an alley mouth.

Silence had returned, and he heard the sound of boots thudding at the far end of the alley. He risked blundering into another gun trap and ran along the alley, his gun uplifted; teeth clenched. The darkness was dense but he kept going until he reached the far end. When he halted all he could hear was his breath rasping in his throat. He strained his ears, and heard running feet off to his left. He went on, hoping to come up with his assailants.

He paused frequently, relying on his ears in the darkness, and finally dropped to one knee when he heard an unseen voice calling in a groaning tone.

'You've gotta help me. I took a slug from that guy. You told me he was good with a gun, but you didn't say he was that good. We had him cold, and you started running at his first shot. Gimme a hand! I've got a slug in the leg and I'm bleeding.'

Arlen heard no reply. He got to his feet and went forward slowly, his gun cocked and ready for action. He paused again when he heard more groaning. Then the voice continued:

'Don't run out on me. Get me to the doc's place. I'm bleeding to death. If you leave me I'll be caught, and that'll lead them to you.'

Boots scraped on hard ground. Arlen started forward, then dropped flat when a gun blasted. He closed his eyes against the flash, and waited until the sounds of the shot faded before getting to his feet. His eyes slowly accustomed themselves to the night and he was able to see something of his surroundings. He covered several yards, and then tripped over an object lying on the ground. He held on to his gun and hit the ground on his right shoulder, rolling several times. His muscles were tensed for the strike of hot lead. He realized that he had tripped over a body, and gritted his teeth as he awaited a violent reaction. When nothing happened he got up and bent over a man stretched lifeless on the ground.

Arlen could feel his heart pounding. He drew a deep breath and bent over the figure, checking it with his left hand, his right holding his pistol ready for any reaction. He pressed his hand against the man's chest, felt the stickiness of blood, but failed to find a heartbeat. He straightened. This was a tough game, he reckoned. Two men had ambushed him right here in town; one had stopped a bullet, and his associate had finished him off to close his mouth permanently.

He remained on one knee, for he could hear the sound of muttered voices in a nearby alley. The gleam of a lantern cut through the darkness, then two men appeared in the alley mouth. Arlen stifled a sigh when he recognized them: the sheriff and his bull-like deputy, Elk Mitchell. Both were holding drawn guns.

'Over here,' Arlen called, and waited for them to arrive.

Mitchell was holding the lantern, and he thrust it towards Arlen's face. Sheriff Floren dropped to one knee beside Arlen, and grabbed Mitchell's wrist to direct the lantern-light on the figure.

'Do you know who he is?' Arlen demanded.

'Yeah, it's Squint Cullen, a local hardcase. I've been meaning to get rid of him. Now he's dead. Did you kill him?'

Arlen gave an account of the incident. Floren arose and Arlen did likewise.

'So there were two of them,' Floren mused. 'Did you get a look at the other one?'

'No. He didn't come close enough for that. But I'm thinking it was the man I'm after.'

'What makes you think that?' Floren's face was grim as he looked at Arlen.

'Cullen called for help, and said that if he was arrested he might lead the law to the other man. That's why he was shot. He's got two bullet wounds; the one that killed him, and the one I gave him – in his leg.

'Did the other guy speak at all? Would you know the sound of Frome's voice if you heard it?'

'No.' Arlen shook his head. 'I've never been this close to him before. But now I know he's in town I'll get him.'

'He'll likely go to ground and stay there,' Floren said. 'Let's go and have a talk with Cullen's wife. She'll know what's going on, and with a bit of luck she might be able to put us on to Frome. Elk, you take care of this end of the deal. Get Charlie Bentford to put Cullen in the mortuary. Tell him I'll see him later. Then go back to the jail. I'll be there in about twenty minutes.'

Mitchell went off with the lamp and Arlen followed Floren. They used another alley to get to the main street. Floren paused, keeping back in the shadows, and subjected the street to an intense scrutiny. Arlen remained silent, content to let the sheriff handle this side of the action.

'I'm wondering where a man like Frome would hide out around here,' Floren mused. 'Do you know enough about him to make a guess?'

'All I know about him is his description,' Arlen said.

'So we'll see Cullen's wife. I've got to break the news about Cullen.'

They walked along the street to the far end of town, where a cluster of shacks and canvas dwellings marked the homes of the poorer townsfolk. Floren paused at a shack where light was issuing from a small window. He rapped on the door and they waited for a reply. Floren rapped again when there was no response, and moments later the door was jerked open and a woman peered out at them. She recognized the sheriff and tried to slam the door, but

40

Floren stuck his boot forward and the door bounced back at her.

'What do you want?' Mrs Cullen demanded. She was tall and thin, with a weathered, unattractive face. Her brown eyes were sharp; filled with suspicion. 'Squint ain't here. He ain't been around in a couple of days.'

'And he ain't coming back,' Floren said brutally. 'He was shot dead in an alley. So what's he been up to? Who's he been running around with?'

'I don't believe you,' she replied. 'What are you trying to pull now?'

'I'll need you to identify his body so you can see for yourself that he's dead. All I'm interested in is arresting the man who killed him.'

'I don't know anything about his business deals. I told you I ain't seen him in several days.'

'The man he was working with is the one who killed him. So start talking. If there's any money on Cullen, you'll wanta get your hands on it, so talk to me and I'll see that you get it. If you don't help me then you won't see a red cent.'

'Squint should have a hundred bucks on him,' she said sharply. 'I saw him counting it this morning, and even he couldn't spend it that quickly.'

'You said you ain't seen him in several days, so quit lying now and tell me the truth.' Floren stepped into the shack and Mrs Cullen retreated before him. 'Where did Cullen pick up a hundred bucks?'

'He was doing a job for a stranger in town who said he was being tailed by a robber and wanted him taken care of.'

'Did you see the stranger? I need to know what he looks like.'

'Small man wearing a good suit and fancy shoes; dark hair and small eyes like a rat – talked different from folks around here. I reckoned he came from back East – New York, I guess. He was a cut above our kind of folk. He had a real big bank roll. You could have choked a cow with it. He was carrying a brown leather bag which he wouldn't put down. I thought he was a whiskey drummer. He looked like he hadn't done a hard day's work in his life. I told Squint not to have anything to do with him because he had a look I didn't cotton to – kind of sly. I didn't believe his story. I reckoned he was lying all along the line.'

'What did he say about being tailed by a robber?' Floren glanced at Arlen as he asked the woman the question. Arlen's eyes were filled with keen anticipation.

'He didn't talk about himself. He said he heard that Squint was a man who fixed things, and he arranged for Squint to meet him on Main Street in front of the hotel around seven o'clock this evening. If the robber showed up in town then they would take him to a quiet place and kill him. Squint left here around six-thirty, and that's the last I saw of him.'

Arlen knew the truth when he heard it, and was satisfied. 'Did you get the name of the stranger?' he asked.

'He didn't say anything about himself.'

'Did he say where he came from?' Arlen persisted.

'Nary a word. He looked like a man with a lot on his mind.'

'Would you know him again if you saw him?' Floren asked.

'I would. So how come you say he killed Squint?'

'I'm checking up on that.' Floren turned to the door. 'I'll come back to you later, Mrs Cullen.'

Arlen preceded Floren out of the shack. The sheriff paused outside.

'I reckon the stranger she described was Frome,' he said.

'There's not much doubt about it,' Arlen agreed. 'That bag he was carrying must contain the money he stole. I can't believe he'd walk around town with it under his arm.'

Floren laughed. 'If he left it in the hotel it would disappear mighty fast.'

'I checked the hotel. The clerk said a man like Frome had been and gone.'

'I'll talk to Hollins. He'll give me the lowdown OK. But I don't reckon Frome would take that dough with him if he set out with Cullen to murder someone. And where is he now?'

'Back in the hotel,' Arlen guessed. 'I doubt he would have booked in normally. He would have paid dough to the clerk and got himself a room without the formalities. He did that in Newton, Kansas.'

'So let's go check out the hotel.' Floren went off at a fast pace and Arlen accompanied him.

The hotel was quiet when they entered. Floren smacked the desk bell with the flat of his hand and the clerk came hurrying out of the back office. He was chewing something, and swallowed quickly when he recognized the sheriff.

'No beating around the bush, Hollins,' Floren said

sharply. 'Where's the little guy who booked in here a few days ago?'

Hollins glanced quickly at Arlen's expressionless face and wiped his mouth with the back of his hand. He shook his head. 'Do you mean the guy this man was asking about earlier?' he demanded.

'I told you to stop beating around the bush,' Floren rasped, his tone turning ugly. 'I'm investigating a murder and I don't have time to waste.'

Hollins looked squarely at Arlen. 'I told you that man left the next morning after booking in, telling me he was heading for Denver, Colorado.'

'He didn't leave,' Floren said. 'How many times did Squint Cullen show up here to see the guy?'

'Cullen?' Hollins shook his head emphatically. 'I wouldn't let him into this hotel even if he offered to pay. He hasn't been around at all.'

'His name wasn't in the register when I looked earlier,' Arlen said.

'He was using the name Foster,' Hollins said.

'You let him stay here for a financial consideration, huh?' Floren demanded. 'That's breaking the law, Hollins. I'd have you in the chain gang for six months if I put you before Judge Talbot. You better come clean and give us the facts straight. Is Foster still in the hotel?'

'I've already said he left for Denver.' Hollins shrugged.

Floren leaned forward across the desk and crashed his right fist against Hollins's jaw. Hollins went over backwards and fell to the floor. He stayed down, shaking his head.

'I knew I wouldn't get a straight answer from you,' Floren observed.

He went around the desk and dragged Hollins to his feet. The door in the back wall opened and a middle-aged woman emerged from the office. She paused at the sight of Hollins sagging in the sheriff's grip, her dark eyes widening.

'What's going on?' she demanded.

'Hollins is going to jail for the night, Mrs Cooper, and he'll spend a lot longer behind bars if he doesn't answer some questions. He's holding out on me.'

'This relates to one of our guests, obviously,' she said. 'Perhaps I can help you.'

Arlen listened while the sheriff explained the situation. He was growing impatient, and wished the sheriff would leave him to make his own investigation. But he was beginning to suspect Floren's motives. The sheriff was just a little too eager to locate Frome, and Arlen assumed that the interest arose from the stolen money Frome was toting around. A warning swirled in the back of his mind. He dropped his right hand to the butt of his holstered gun and let it remain motionless with the butt touching the inside of his wrist, although he did not think the situation would devolve into shooting – yet.

'We don't need answers, Sheriff,' Arlen said. 'All we've got to do is search the hotel. If Frome is here then we'll find him.'

Floren paused, holding the semi-conscious Hollins upright while he considered Arlen's words. Then he nodded and let the clerk drop to the floor.

'Come on,' Floren said. 'I know this place. Just follow me.' He started forward, and then paused and looked at Mrs Cooper. 'Give me a key that will unlock all the guest rooms,' he rapped.

Mrs Cooper sighed audibly and opened a drawer in the reception desk. She produced a key and handed it to Floren. 'Please be as quiet as you can,' she said. 'Try not to disturb the guests unduly.'

Floren led the way to the stairs and they ascended. At the top there was a corridor running right to left with doors opening off it on either side. Floren tapped on the first door on the right, which was opened by a woman. He entered the room and looked around, found no sign of a man, and continued to the second door. Arlen followed silently; he watched the sheriff search every room without success before reaching the room at the front of the hotel, overlooking the street.

Arlen was at Floren's shoulder when the sheriff tried to unlock the last door, but the key would not enter the lock.

'Someone's inside,' Floren rasped, and pounded on the centre panel with heavy knuckles.

The door was jerked open and a big man appeared. He was over six feet tall, well-muscled and smoothly fleshed. His face was large, almost shapeless, his forehead broad. Dark eyes peered from under black brows, and a black, flowing moustache was like a stain under his broad nose. He was in his late forties.

'What do you want?' he demanded.

'Mr Sandor!' Floren's tone rapidly changed from bluster to fawning politeness. 'I didn't know you were still in the hotel.'

Arlen snapped to full alertness. The name Sandor was familiar, and he studied the big man while searching his mind for details. Then it came to him. Rufus Sandor was the mystery man who had sent two hardcases to deliver a message to Brenda Farrell, ordering her father to visit him here at the hotel later in the week.

'We're searching for a man, Mr Sandor,' Floren said respectfully. 'I need to check out this room.'

Sandor opened the door wide and stepped back. 'OK,' he said. 'Do it quick, and then get to hell out of here.'

Floren entered the room. Sandor stood motionless, his gaze on Arlen's face. Arlen heard an inner door slam as Floren checked a second room.

'You're a stranger in town.' Sandor's eyes were intent as he gazed at Arlen.

'Just like you,' Arlen replied.

Floren emerged from the room, smiling, and almost bowed to Sandor.

'Sorry you've been troubled, Mr Sandor,' he said.

Sandor did not reply. He slammed the door, and Arlen heard the sound of a key being turned on the inside. As they returned to the reception desk, Arlen said:

'Who is that guy?'

'You wanta stay well away from him,' Floren replied in a low tone. 'He's a big man from back East, and he's got half a dozen tough men travelling with him. He's been here more than a week, and I'll be damned glad when he moves on.'

'Did he report to you when he arrived?' Arlen demanded, and laughed softly when Floren cursed inaudibly instead of answering. 'What line of business is he in?' he continued.

'Everything that shows a profit, I reckon.' Floren shrugged. 'He's a real bad man, and it ain't wise to tangle

47

with his kind.'

'What's he after around here?' Arlen persisted. When Floren did not reply, he changed the subject 'What are you gonna do about those two hardcases I tangled with earlier?'

'I'll know more about that after I've spoken to Brenda Farrell again. I'll be seeing her tomorrow. If they did try to rob her then I'll throw the book at them.'

'Are they under arrest?'

'Sure they are. I've put them behind bars for the time being. What kind of a law department do you think I run here?'

Arlen shook his head. 'I'd like to have a few words with them,' he said.

'Sure. Why not? Come along to the office. Did the Farrell girl say anything more about the hold-up incident while you were with her?'

'Not a word.' Arlen pictured Brenda's face and an unaccustomed wave of emotion darted through his breast. He compressed his lips and fought against his feelings. Nothing mattered in this county except the capture of Alec Frome. He had to keep his attention focused on that one clear point.

He followed Floren across the street to the law office. Floren paused before opening the door. He sighed heavily and turned slowly, as if trying to reach a firm decision about some problem.

'I need to see Charlie Bentford, the undertaker, before I do anything else,' he said. 'Come with me. Elk won't let you see the prisoners until he gets an OK from me, so you'll be wasting your time unless I'm there.'

Arlen followed the sheriff. They went along the sidewalk and entered an alley just past the livery stable. Arlen tensed as they passed into almost total darkness, and followed Floren by sound until they emerged on the back lots, where a light in a low building near by gave them some faint illumination. Floren led the way into a low building.

They entered a long room which was sparsely furnished: a few cupboards on a wall, two small tables at the far end, a paper-strewn desk, and in the centre of the floor space a long table on which lay the stripped cadaver of Squint Cullen. A small, thin man, stoop-shouldered and shaggy-haired, was bent over the corpse; he straightened when Floren called out to him. He turned and limped forward a couple of steps, then paused, shaking his head, before returning his attention to the dead man.

'Who killed Cullen, Sheriff?' he demanded.

'That ain't none of your concern, Charlie, Just tell me what you found on him.'

'What are you looking for?' Bentford countered.

'Have you searched him yet?' Floren demanded impatiently.

'I ain't had time. I've only just stripped him.' Bentford shrugged. 'Have you caught the killer yet?'

'No; it's early days.' Floren went to a pile of discarded clothes and searched the pockets. When he found nothing of interest he turned to the undertaker. 'Cullen had a hundred bucks on him this morning,' he said, 'and he ain't got it now.'

'What's that got to do with me?' Bentford glanced sideways at Floren, his expression changing.

49

'Someone's got it,' Floren said doggedly. 'I reckon it was on him when he was shot dead.'

'Well don't look at me.' Bentford thrust out his chin. 'Maybe the guy that shot him took it.'

Floren glanced at Arlen, who shook his head.

'Then again,' Bentford continued, 'Elk fetched me to collect the body, and he was alone with Cullen. Maybe he helped himself, huh?'

'Elk knows better than that,' Floren growled. 'But I'll talk to him.'

Arlen sighed impatiently. He wanted to get away from Floren, feeling that the lawman was staying with him just to keep abreast of the situation, which indicated that he was afraid that he might miss something. Arlen wondered what kind of law Floren was dispensing in the county. But he shrugged aside his doubts for they did not involve his business. He wanted Alec Frome and the stolen bank money, and when he had successfully completed his case he would shake the dust of Nebraska from his boots.

'I wonder where the hundred bucks went?' Floren mused as they walked back to the law office.

Arlen did not reply. He was thinking that the money would have disappeared into Floren's pocket if it had not already been taken. When they entered the office Elk Mitchell sprang to his feet from the chair behind the littered desk. He moved aside and stood motionless.

'What have you done with the hundred bucks Cullen had on him?' Floren asked.

'It's right here.' Elk smirked and pointed to a pile of bills on the desk. 'I found the dough when I searched

Cullen, and reckoned you wouldn't want to put temptation in Bentford's way.'

Floren grinned and picked up the money. He counted
it, before slipping it into a breast pocket.

'I'll see that Mrs Cullen gets it,' he said. 'Now you want
to talk to Darley and Gauvin, huh, Arlen? I doubt you'll
get anything out of them, but go ahead through that door.
They're in the cells back there.'

Arlen was surprised when Floren did not accompany
him. He entered the cell block and saw the two men who
had attacked Brenda Farrell together in a cell. He studied
them for a moment while they regarded him with sullen
defiance in their narrowed eyes.

'Which one of you is Darley?' Arlen demanded.

'I am.' One of the pair got up from the bunk on which
he had been lying and came to the door. He was dressed
in a town suit of near-black colour, and wore a string tie on
his white shirt. His face was filled with aggression and his
brown eyes glinted with menace. He looked what he was:
a hired hardcase with no compunction and even less
mercy in his nature. 'I told you earlier that we weren't
robbing that gal. We had a message for her father.'

'It took two of you to deliver a message to a girl?' Arlen
said scornfully.

'That's the way we work. We wasn't gonna harm her.'

'When I came up you had a knife at her throat,' Arlen
recalled. 'Is that the way you usually deliver a message?'

'She was getting fractious and I was trying to calm her
down.'

'Why does Sandor wanta talk to Buck Farrell?'

A smile flitted across Darley's face but vanished in an

instant. 'I reckon you better see Mr Sandor about that,' he said glibly.

'And I'd like to be there when you do it,' Gauvin said.

Arlen transferred his attention to Gauvin, who was lounging on a bunk. The right leg of his pants was blood-stained above the knee and had been slit open. The limb had been bandaged.

'Why did you run away if you were only delivering a message?'

'You didn't have to shoot me,' Gauvin growled.

'It looked like you were robbing that young woman, so I dealt with you accordingly. You're a couple of hardcases, and I hope the local law puts you out of circulation for a long time.'

'We'll be outa here first thing in the morning,' Darley rasped.

Arlen turned away, aware that he would learn nothing from the pair. He went back into the front office. Elk Mitchell had departed. Floren was seated at his desk.

'You seemed keen not to upset Sandor in the hotel,' Arlen said. 'Why did he get special treatment?'

Floren shrugged. 'Not that it's any of your business, but I've been the sheriff here for a long time, and I've developed an instinct for handling people. That's the way I see Sandor. I need to find out what he's up to around here, and if I used strong-arm tactics on him I'd soon find myself up to my neck in big trouble.'

'Has he ever been in this neck of the woods before?'

'No. But I sure as hell would like to know what he's up to. You're going out to look for Frome now, I guess?'

Arlen nodded. 'That's right. I wasted some valuable

time tracking around with you.'

He departed before Floren could decide what to do, and walked away from the office quickly. He moved along the sidewalk to the nearest alley, slipped into its cover and remained motionless, watching the law office. He wanted to know what the sheriff would decide to do. What he didn't need was the lawman breathing down his neck while he hunted Frome.

A moment later he saw Floren leave the office and head away along the street in the direction of the shack where Mrs Cullen lived. Arlen went along to the saloon, feeling the need of a drink, aware that there was nothing he could do about Frome before morning. He peered into the saloon over the batwings, checking the crowd inside before venturing across the threshold. His gaze fell immediately upon a small man standing at the far end of the bar. His surprise was complete when he recognized Alec Frome by his clothes.

He entered the saloon and strode along the bar, his concentration on the fugitive. Frome glanced in Arlen's direction, turned instantly and darted to his left before lunging through an open doorway that gave access to the private rooms at the rear. Arlen dashed forward, dropping a hand to his gun. Then someone standing at the bar stuck out a foot and tripped him. He fell heavily. He rolled and started to his feet, but a gun butt thudded against his skull and he felt as if the roof had fallen in on him. Blackness swooped into his brain and his face hit the floor as he lost consciousness.

FOUR

Arlen regained his senses to find himself lying on his back with a bartender standing over him, pouring a jug of water on his face. He sat up quickly and the big room seemed to tilt crazily. He lowered his chin to his chest and closed his eyes until the gyrations ceased. A big hand grasped him under the right arm and hauled him to his feet. He opened his eyes and looked into the grinning face of Elk Mitchell. The deputy supported him until he could stand without assistance.

'Who hit me?' Arlen demanded.

Mitchell's grin widened as he pointed to a man stretched out on the floor. 'I got to him just too late to stop him. He sure tried to crack your skull.'

'Did you see Frome run out through that back door?' Arlen demanded.

Mitchell's face took on a scowl. He gazed at Arlen for a moment, as if his brain could not make sense of Arlen's words. Then he became animated.

'Frome?' he growled. 'That's the guy with the bank dough!'

He ran to the back door, crashed through it, and Arlen heard him in the back room, using brute strength to get out of the saloon. The bartender handed Arlen a towel, and he sat down on the nearest chair and mopped his face, temporarily unable to take up the chase. But he was far from unhappy. Frome was still around. The trail was not cold.

The man who had struck Arlen came to his senses and got to his feet. Arlen drew his gun and made him sit on the floor with his back to the bar and his hands on his head. Ten minutes later Mitchell returned with a scowl on his large face. The big deputy went to the bar and called for whiskey. He looked at Arlen, still seated, and cursed.

'I didn't see hide or hair of Frome,' he reported. 'He sure is a fast mover.'

'At least we know he's still in town,' Arlen commented. He pointed to the man sitting on the floor. 'Who is he?' he demanded.

'Joe Reece – one of Rufus Sandor's men.'

'And do you let him get away with what he did?'

'Hell, no! You make a charge against him and I'll put him behind bars. He'll come up in front of Judge Talbot and we'll have him in the chain gang for six months.'

Arlen doubted that, judging by the way Floren had fawned around Sandor in the hotel earlier. 'OK,' he said. 'I'll charge him with assault and causing bodily harm. Jail him now. I'll drop in at the office in the morning and sign the charge.'

Mitchell departed with the prisoner. Arlen got to his feet, took a couple of experimental steps, and then continued to the batwings. He left the saloon and went to the livery barn. He entered cautiously, for stables were notorious places for ambush and robbery. He found the interior gloomy, with only one lantern alight near the main entrance. There was a dim light in the small office, and he approached it silently. Joe Henty was inside, asleep and snoring with his head cushioned on his arms on the dusty desk. Arlen knocked loudly on the door. Henty snorted, opened his eyes and then sat up. He pulled a silver pocket watch out of a breast pocket, consulted it, then got to his feet.

'It's time I went for my supper and then hit the sack,' he observed.

'Before you go, tell me if you've seen the man I'm looking for,' Arlen said, and described Frome.

'Say, I remember him – a little guy that looked like he belonged in a big city back East. He was carrying a leather bag. Yeah, he was in here about two hours ago. He first rode into town about four days ago on a chestnut that was on its last legs. Earlier this evening he dropped in to buy a fresh animal; said he was leaving first thing tomorrow morning for Denver, Colorado.'

'Show me the horse he bought,' Arlen said.

'OK. It's over there.'

Henty led the way and paused at a stall containing a black horse. Arlen studied the animal, liking its lines. Frome certainly knew horseflesh! This animal would run all day.

'Do you know where the guy is staying in town?' Arlen asked.

'The hotel, I guess.' Henty grimaced.

Arlen departed and went to the hotel. The reception

area was deserted. He rang the bell and waited, but no one answered. He went behind the desk and picked up his key from the board. As he ascended the stairs, Rufus Sandor appeared above him and came down hurriedly, followed by a hard-faced man wearing two guns at his waist. Sandor looked right through Arlen as they passed on the stairs, and continued without pause. The accompanying gunman gave Arlen the once-over with dark, expression-less eyes.

Arlen was tempted to follow them, but thought better of it and went to his room. He turned in with a sigh of relief and slept fitfully until dawn. As soon as he awoke he left the hotel by the back stairs and crossed the back lots to the livery barn. The town was still sleeping, but there was some activity in the stable. Arlen entered by the back door and stood still for some moments, listening intently. He could hear someone saddling up and talking to the horse.

There was a small figure in the stall containing the horse that Frome had bought, and Arlen could not believe his luck as he drew his gun and edged forward. He recog-nized Frome from the description he had been given, and watched the little man struggling to lift a saddle on to the back of the horse. The leather case that Frome never let out of his sight was standing on the ground just inside the stall.

Frome had his back to Arlen, who sneaked forward and picked up the case. Frome caught a glimpse of his move-ment and swung around as if he had been shot. His reflexes were good because he overcame his surprise and reached inside his jacket to grasp the butt of a gun nestling in his left armpit.

'Pull the gun and I'll shoot you in the gut,' Arlen warned.

Frome stopped his movement, desperation showing in his face.

'You've got good sense,' Arlen observed.

Frome raised his hands. He was barely five foot six in height, small boned and thin. His face showed more than his fifty years. He looked at Arlen, heaved a sigh, and then seemed to shrink within himself.

'Who are you?' he demanded in a husky voice. 'Where did you come from?'

'I've trailed you all the way from the bank where you stole the money.' Arlen shook the case. 'How much is left? You led me quite a dance across Kansas. But you didn't really think you'd get away with it, did you?'

Frome did not answer. He glanced around desperately, but there was no escape.

'Get rid of your gun now,' Arlen told him. 'Do it slowly. Use your index finger and thumb. Take it out and drop it on the ground. Your trip to Denver is cancelled. Why did you head up this way? Who do you know around here?'

'I don't know anyone.' Frome shook his head. 'I was being chased by the law, and I hoped to throw you off my trail.'

'You're lying,' Arlen said. 'I was told that you came from this town when you first went to Dodge City to work in the bank. So what happened to you, Frome? Twenty years working with a good record, and then you up and steal ten thousand bucks.'

Frome did not reply. He disarmed himself and dropped

the gun on the ground. He seemed resigned to the situation.

'What happens now?' he asked.

'I'll put you in the local jail, send a wire to your bank and my agency informing them that I've got you and have what's left of the stolen dough. Then I'll deposit the money in the local bank. In a few days we'll start the trip back to Dodge.'

'Are you a lawman?'

'I'm a Butterworth detective.' Arlen smiled briefly.

'That's just my luck.' Frome sighed heavily.

Arlen shrugged. 'Butterfield's motto is: "We always get our man!" That's true in your case. Come on. You know where the jail is. Head for it and don't try to give me any trouble.'

The sun was beginning to show over the eastern horizon as they walked along the main street. The town was still asleep, but Sheriff Floren was at his desk when Arlen ushered Frome into the law office. Floren did a double take when he saw Frome, and his eyes gleamed momentarily. He looked at Arlen before switching his gaze to the case Arlen had taken from Frome.

'Is that Frome?' Floren demanded. 'Where did you pick him up? Have you got the stolen money? How much dough is there?'

'Go easy on the questions,' Arlen said. 'Lock him in a cell while I do some checking.'

Floren picked up the jail keys from a corner of the desk and jerked a thumb at the door that led into the cells. Frome walked dejectedly across the office. Arlen heaved a sigh and dumped the case on the desk. When he opened

59

it he saw that Frome had not spent a great deal of the stolen money. He counted it quickly, discovering that only a couple of hundred dollars was missing from the original $10,000.

Floren emerged from the cell block and dropped the keys on the desk. He gazed intently at the pile of greenbacks on the desk, and grimaced when Arlen began replacing them in the case.

'Is it all there?' Floren demanded.

'A couple of hundred bucks are missing.' Arlen picked up the case. 'I'll be back later to question Frome. I expect we'll be heading back to Dodge tomorrow.'

'What are you gonna do with that money?'

'Do with it?' Arlen grinned. 'What do you think? I'm gonna stick it in the local bank and get a receipt for it. I'm not gonna carry it all the way back with me. It might give some undesirables a temptation they might find hard to resist.'

Floren's face was expressionless as Arlen crossed to the street door. 'You better be on your guard while you're in town,' he suggested.

Arlen smiled. 'I thought you kept a tight grip on the lawlessness around here.'

He went back to the hotel, ate breakfast in the dining room, and then stayed in his room until it was time to visit the bank. The town had come to life when he eventually went out to the street, and he was fully alert as he headed for the bank. A man dressed in a fine town suit, with a red bow tie at his throat, was unlocking the bank door as Arlen arrived. He glanced at Arlen, and his blue eyes crinkled as he called a greeting.

'Good morning. You're early, aren't you?'

'Special business,' Arlen replied. He lifted the case. 'There's almost ten thousand bucks in here – stolen from a bank in Dodge City. I arrested the robber this morning, and I'd like to deposit the recovered money with you.'

'It will be a pleasure to do business with you. I'm John Roarke, the banker.'

'I'm Jeff Arlen, a detective for the Butterworth Detective Agency, Chicago.'

'I'm pleased to meet you, Mr Arlen.' Roarke offered his hand. 'Did you trail the robber all the way from Dodge?'

'He had me worried a couple of times, but I finally caught up with him this morning.'

They entered the bank and Arlen was relieved when the money was safely in the bank vault. He checked the receipt and handed it back to Roarke.

'Send that by mail today. Address it to the Butterworth Detective Agency in Chicago.'

'It will go out on the midnight express tonight,' Roarke told him.

Arlen felt as if a great load had been lifted from his shoulders as he left the bank. Now all he had to do was get Frome back to the scene of his crime.

He went back to the jail to question Frome, and found Elk Mitchell in the cell block giving Frome a hard time. The cell door was open and Mitchell was inside, standing over Frome, who was huddled semi-conscious on the floor with blood dribbling from a cut over his right eye. There was no sign of the sheriff.

'What's going on?' Arlen demanded, and Mitchell's head swivelled round on his thick neck. 'Get the hell out of there,' continued Arlen furiously. 'That's my prisoner you're handling, and I'm telling you now that you don't question him or lay a finger on him. Is that clear?'

'He's in our jail, and that puts him under our jurisdiction,' replied Mitchell in a rough tone. 'He's a criminal, and I wanta know what he's doing in this town. Don't try and tell me my job, mister.'

'I'm not gonna tell you anything.' Arlen smiled. 'I've told you once to stay away from Frome and I won't repeat the warning. Step over the line again where Frome is concerned and I'll take your badge and push it down your throat.'

Mitchell bristled. 'You can't talk to me like that, mister,' he snarled.

'I've finished talking. Step out of line again and you'll discover how we do things in Chicago.'

'You're maybe forgetting that you're a long way from Chicago,' Mitchell responded. He emerged from the cell and turned to lock the door.

'Leave it,' Arlen told him. 'Give me the keys and get to hell out of here.'

Mitchell glared at him for several tense moments, then tossed the bunch of keys to him. Arlen caught them deftly and waited until Mitchell had departed. Then he entered the cell and bent over Frome.

'Are you badly hurt?' he demanded.

Frome shook his head and sat up. 'I'm OK,' he said.

'You're in a bad spot. Not only are you facing a charge of embezzlement from your bank, there's also the question of the murder of Squint Cullen, and that is the local sheriff's domain. Why did you shoot Cullen? I shot him in the leg, and you went back to him when he called to you for help and shot him dead.'

'I don't know anyone called Cullen.' Frome shook his head.

'Let's get one thing straight right now,' Arlen told him. 'I know when you lie to me, and I don't like it. So let's start as we mean to go on. I'll ask questions and you give me truthful answers. That way we can iron out all our problems before we head back to Dodge. So let's start again. Why did you kill Cullen?'

Frome remained silent. Arlen studied him for several moments, fighting down his impatience. He realized that he would get no cooperation from his prisoner but he suppressed a sigh and made another attempt.

'You've stated that you don't know Cullen, but I have a witness who has described you and saw you give Cullen one hundred bucks yesterday morning, saying it was payment for helping him stop a robber trailing you. I guess you were talking about me, seeing that you and Cullen ambushed me on the street last night, and I reckon you knew I was a detective on your tail. The witness is Mrs Cullen. Now make a statement giving the facts of your meeting with Cullen, and why you killed him.'

Frome compressed his lips and gazed defiantly at Arlen. A fly buzzed loudly at the window of the cell, and Frome started nervously. Arlen waited a couple of minutes in deep silence, giving Frome time to consider his position. When he was satisfied that Frome was not going to answer he left the cell, locked the door, and stood motionless, gazing at Frome. Again there was no reaction from the man, Arlen turned away and went back into the office.

The sheriff was at his desk and Mitchell was not present. Floren leaned back in his seat and gazed at Arlen, who paused beside the desk. An eager glint showed in the sheriff's eyes, and Arlen suspected that he would have trouble over the stolen money.

'Mitchell was giving Frome a rough time, Sheriff,' Arlen said. 'I warned him off, but that may not be enough. Tell him to lay off – no questions about the stolen money, or anything else for that matter, except Cullen's murder. That's your business, and I'm aware that Frome will have to remain here to face a charge of murder if you can prove that he killed Cullen.'

'He'll be treated according to the law,' Floren said. 'I've got enough evidence to hold him on a charge of murdering Cullen, and as that takes precedence over any other charges, including embezzlement, I'm going ahead on the murder. You won't be taking Frome back to Dodge City at all. He'll stand trial here, and if he gets off the murder charge then you can have him, but I've got a good case against him. Your evidence alone will hang him.'

'I know Frome killed Cullen,' Arlen said sharply, 'but I didn't see him do it. All I can testify to is that the man with Cullen fired the fatal shot. That's not enough to prove him guilty.'

'Mrs Cullen's evidence, coupled with yours, will do the trick.' Floren got to his feet. He held out his hand and Arlen stared at him.

'What do you want?' Arlen demanded.

'The receipt you got from the bank for the money you paid in.'

Arlen shook his head. 'I don't think so,' he said. 'You're

not charging Frome with embezzlement. That charge will stand alone until after the murder trial.'

'It will be brought to the notice of the judge, and he'll want the dough as evidence.'

'I'll telegraph my head office for their instructions,' Arlen said firmly.

He left the office and walked along the street, considering the situation. The more he saw of Floren and Mitchell the more convinced he became that they were not to be trusted. He saw the telegraph office on a corner and went to it, composed a report, and sent it to the Butterworth Agency in Chicago. With this accomplished, he had nothing to do but wait for a reply and fresh orders. He recalled that Brenda Farrell was coming into town around noon to see him, and checked the time. He had an hour to wait for the girl's arrival, and he went into the saloon for a beer.

The big room in the saloon was practically deserted. Three men were seated at one of the small tables, engrossed in a game of poker, and Arlen wondered if they had been playing through the night. A bartender was busy cleaning the bar top. He looked up at Arlen's approach, his expression showing annoyance.

'I ain't open yet,' he snapped.

'You ain't closed,' retorted Arlen, jerking a thumb at the gamblers. 'Give me a beer.'

The bartender opened his mouth to refuse, but noted Arlen's expression and shrugged. He filled a glass with foaming beer and slid it along the bar. Arlen saw that the glass was mostly foam, He waited until the foam lost its agitation and reverted to liquid, which filled the glass only three-quarters full, and then sent the glass sliding back along the bar to where the bartender was standing.

'Top it up, and this time do it properly,' Arlen rapped.

The bartender repeated the operation and Arlen slapped a silver coin on the bar. As he raised the glass to his lips he became aware of a figure moving up beside him. He drank a mouthful of beer and set down the glass before looking at the newcomer. The man was dressed in a black outfit and had two pistols holstered on his slim hips. Arlen recognized him as the man who had accompanied Rufus Sandor out of the hotel the previous evening.

'You're Arlen, the Butterworth detective, ain't you?' the man demanded. 'I'm Jethro Bain, and I got a message for you. Mr Sandor wants to see you now at the hotel.'

'I've got no business with Sandor,' Arlen replied. 'So what if I refuse to see him?'

'I was told to give you the message. What you do about it is up to you. If you don't go to see him and I get an order to fetch you then that's what I'll do.'

'You might have some difficulty in handling that chore.' Arlen drained his glass and put it down on the bar. He turned and left the saloon, pausing outside on the boardwalk to see if the gunman would follow him.

The batwings remained closed, and Arlen heaved a sigh. He looked around the quiet street. The storekeeper was in front of his place, sweeping yesterday's dust from the boards in front of his window. A townsman was already seated on one of the two chairs to the right of the store doorway. A man was standing in an alley mouth opposite the saloon, his right hand close to the butt of his holstered gun, and he looked as if he were ready for some kind of action. On the near side of the street another man was leaning a shoulder against an awning post by the hotel entrance, and he had the same kind of eagerness in his attitude.

Trouble waiting to happen for someone, Arlen thought, able to read the signs. His eyes narrowed when he saw the sheriff emerge from the law office. Floren paused to hitch up his gunbelt before crossing the street. He paused when he reached the opposite sidewalk, took a quick look around and then entered the bank. Arlen heaved a sigh. The local law seemed very interested in the money Frome had stolen.

Jethro Bain emerged from the saloon and went on to the hotel without looking at Arlen, who remained motionless until the gunman had entered the hotel before moving in the same direction. He estimated that he had under an hour to kill before Brenda Farrell arrived in town, and he was curious about Sandor. He was aware that something was going on beneath the surface of town life and guessed it involved Buck Farrell and his daughter.

When he entered the hotel, Arlen saw Bain standing at the reception desk talking to Hollins, who was badly bruised around the left eye. Neither man looked at him as he passed them, but Bain called to him before he reached the foot of the stairs. Arlen did not pause, but he was tensed and ready for trouble.

'If you're going up to see Mr Sandor then you'd better leave your gun down here, Arlen,' Bain advised.

'I don't walk around town naked,' Arlen responded. He went up to Sandor's room and knocked on the door.

A big man opened the door. He was dressed in a grey

town suit, and there was a bulge at his left armpit. His jacket was open and his right hand was tense at his waist. He studied Arlen for a moment, his blue eyes intent, and then he looked over his shoulder and said:

'It's the detective, Mr Sandor.'

'Let him in,' Sandor replied.

The door was opened wider and Arlen entered. His gun was whipped out of its holster as he passed the gunman, and when he swung round the man grinned.

'You'll get it back when you leave,' he said.

Sandor was standing by the window, peering down at the street. Arlen walked to his side and looked down at the alley opposite. The man standing there was still alert and looking around, his right hand close to his holstered gun.

'You look like you're watching for something to happen,' Arlen said.

Sandor looked at him with dark, searching eyes, and the hint of a grin touched his thin lips before flitting away, almost before Arlen saw it.

'So you spotted that man in the alley opposite, huh?' Sandor nodded.

'And the second one on this side of the street near the hotel,' Arlen added.

'They told me you are a good detective.'

'Who told you that?'

'You wouldn't know if I told you. Thank you for coming. I didn't think you would. But you being here points to one thing – you're interested in my presence in town and you want to know more.'

Arlen did not take his eyes off the man in the alley mouth. He said: 'So what's of interest around here?'

'It's business. That's all I can tell you. I do have a personal interest, but that's private.'

'You sent two men to give a message to Brenda Farrell
last night. I heard her protest and went to see what was
going on. Your men were attacking her. One had hold of
her arms from behind and the other was in front of her,
with a knife at her throat. I went to her aid, and afterwards
saw her home. I thought she was being robbed, and couldn't
believe it when she said your men were giving her a
message. What kind of people do you employ?'

'I shall deal with them when they get out of jail,' Sandor
said. 'They overstepped the mark, and they'll pay for that.'

'They may be behind bars for a very long time,' Arlen
observed. 'My evidence against them could get them five
years apiece.'

'It would be better if you dropped any charges you
might have made against them.' Sandor heaved an
audible sigh. 'Your only interest in that business is the
welfare of Miss Farrell, and you'll be acting against her
interests if you don't stay out of it.'

'I don't see it like that. What happened last night left a
nasty taste in my mouth. Not only am I a Butterworth
detective, I'm also a deputy US marshal.'

'So you have other reasons for being here than the
apprehension of Frome.' Sandor nodded. 'Am I the real
reason why you're in town?'

'I don't know a thing about you, Sandor, and I don't
wish to know.'

Arlen had not taken his eyes off the man in the alley
mouth. He saw the sheriff return across the street and
enter the law office. The waiting man glanced around the

street and then drew his pistol. He looked up at the window where Arlen was standing, lifted his gun, and triggered the weapon. Arlen acted instinctively. He thrust Sandor away from the window as he dived to the floor. The next instant he heard the sound of shots, and shattered glass showered over him from the broken window.

FIVE

Arlen stayed down until the shooting ceased. Sandor did not move. He was standing by the front wall, clear of the window, where Arlen had pushed him. As the gun echoes faded Arlen got to his feet and looked out of the window. The man in the alley mouth had gone, and a haze of gunsmoke was drifting across the street from where he had been standing. Arlen glanced at Sandor. A trace of blood showed on Sandor's forehead where he had been caught by a flying shard of glass. Sandor motioned to his gunman, who threw Arlen's pistol on the floor and departed quickly.

'You moved fast,' Sandor observed, producing a handkerchief and dabbing at his forehead. 'Thanks for saving my life.'

'Who was he shooting at?' Arlen countered. 'Was it you or me?'

'It was you, I suppose.' Sandor shook his head. He appeared to be completely unruffled by the incident. 'I don't have any enemies around here.'

'And you think I do?' Arlen shrugged. 'Was he one of

your men?'

'I never saw him before. And do you think I would organize something like this?'

'Where are your men? Shouldn't they be covering the hotel while you're in it? You strike me as a man who would have a lot of enemies, and you do have six hardcases looking out for your interests.'

'You've been checking up on me.' Sandor shook his head and smiled. 'Are you having any luck in your search for Frome?'

'I arrested him last night. He's in jail now, waiting to be taken back to Dodge.'

Sandor's face did not change expression. He asked: 'Did you recover the money?'

'All of it except two hundred bucks.'

'And you've put that in the local bank, I guess.' Sandor nodded. 'That's what I would have done had I been in your boots.'

'I came here at your request.' Arlen's patience was running out. 'So why do you want to see me?'

Sandor turned away from the window and went to a leather easy chair across the room. He poured a whiskey from a bottle on a nearby table and took a drink.

'Help yourself if you'd like a drink,' he invited.

'No thanks. I expect to be busy this morning, and I'll need a clear head.'

'I wanted to warn you against the local lawmen,' Sandor said. 'They're as crooked as hell!'

'I've already worked that out for myself.'

'They're not going to let you take the stolen money back to Chicago.'

'That might prove to be a chore beyond their abilities.'

'You can't fight against a bullet in the back.' Sandor smiled. 'They'll go that far to get what they want. I can tell that you haven't come up against their set-up yet. If you had you would have upped stakes last night as soon as you arrested Frome. Now I fear you've left it too late to pull out.'

Arlen looked at the shattered window. 'Was that shooting at us part of whatever Floren is working on?'

'All I know is that the gunman was not one of my men.'

Arlen went back to the window and looked down at the street. There was a crowd of men standing on the opposite sidewalk, looking around and talking loudly. There was no sign of the sheriff or his deputy, and he would have expected them to be at the scene. Their absence seemed to corroborate Sandor's accusation. He went back to confront Sandor, bent to pick up his gun, and returned it to his holster.

'Thanks for the warning,' Arlen said. 'I have to get moving. I'll maybe see you around, huh?'

'It's likely that you'll come to me for help before this is over,' Sandor replied.

'You're talking but you ain't saying anything.' Arlen waited for a reply but Sandor merely shrugged.

Arlen's patience ran out then and he left the room. When he reached the lobby he found Hollins alone behind the desk. The clerk glanced up as Arlen went to the street door, and turned away to avoid speaking. The crowd around the alley mouth opposite was dispersing. Sheriff Floren was on the scene now, and his harsh voice chivvied the crowd. Arlen went to Floren's side, and was greeted with a smile.

'Did you get a good look at the gunman?' Floren demanded.

'Just as good as you did.' Arlen suppressed a sigh. 'You saw him when you left your office to visit the bank, and again when you went back to your office.'

'Who was he shooting at?' Floren glanced around the street. 'You weren't around so it wasn't you.'

Arlen related the incident and Floren's bronzed features seemed to pale. His eyes narrowed and he looked up at the window of Sandor's hotel room. Arlen laughed drily.

'You'd better go up there and talk to Sandor,' he suggested. 'I probably saved his life, but you weren't around, so you'll have some fast talking to do.'

'I've got a description of the man who did the shooting, and I wanta look around town quick before he beats it. You're getting friendly with Sandor, ain't you?'

'Not so you'd notice. He sent for me.'

'What did he want with you?'

'He didn't say.' Arlen heard the sound of approaching hoofs and glanced around to see Brenda Farrell coming into town. 'How's my prisoner this morning?'

'In the same condition you left him last night.' Floren grasped Arlen's arm. 'I'll need a statement from you about what happened here. Drop into the office sometime today, huh?'

'I'll be around,' Arlen told him, and went along the street towards the approaching girl.

'Good morning,' he called as Brenda reined in at the stable door and dismounted.

'Good morning,' she replied. 'Has something happened

around here?'

'Why do you ask?' He studied her face.

She seemed pensive, and her eyes proclaimed that she was afraid. She let her horse drink at the trough. Arlen waited silently until the animal had taken its fill, and followed when Brenda led it into the stable. He explained the shooting at the hotel while she unsaddled the horse, and she stopped and gazed at him, her expression changing as she heard him out.

'So that was why there was a crowd along the street. Did the sheriff catch the man who did the shooting?'

Arlen shook his head.

'But you saw the man.' She looked into Arlen's face as if trying to read his mind. 'Can you describe him?'

'Do you think you might know him?'

'It's likely. I know most people in town.'

'I saw him standing in the alley mouth as I went to the hotel,' Arlen mused. 'In my job, if you don't notice things like that you get caught flat-footed. He was in his twenties, about six feet, dark eyes and hair. He was wearing a blue shirt and a yellow neckerchief, denim pants, crossed cartridge belts containing two pistols, and riding boots.'

'You saw plenty with just a glance,' she observed.

'It's a habit,' Arlen told her.

'You'd better talk to Henty. He'd know something about him if he left a horse here.'

'Have you any idea who it might be?' he asked.

She shook her head. Arlen was considering how lovely she was. There was a certain light in her eyes, and she did not seem at all troubled by what had happened to her when she had been accosted the previous evening by

Sandor's two men. When she did not reply to his question he moistened his lips.

'There's a sparkle about you this morning. Has something happened out at the ranch?'

'I'm feeling optimistic, that's all. My father assures me that there is no trouble.'

'What about those two men who accosted you last evening?'

She shrugged. 'Dad says he'll talk to Mr Sandor about them. I've come in this morning to tell you that there's nothing to worry about.'

'What about Jake Pearson? Did your father convince you that he was not acting badly last night? And let us not forget the night riders.'

'Dad said he'd handle everything when he sees Mr Sandor later.'

'So Mr Sandor has all the answers,' Arlen mused. 'Have you ever heard of a man called Alec Frome? He worked in a Dodge City bank for twenty years, but lived around here before then.'

Brenda blinked at the mention of the name and Arlen felt a slight feathery sensation come to life in his breast. But she shook her head.

'I don't think I've heard that name,' she replied.

Arlen sensed that she was lying but said nothing more.

'I'm sorry I wasted your time last night,' she said slowly.

'It wasn't wasted. In fact it was most interesting. You knew a man called Squint Cullen, I expect?'

'Everyone knows Cullen. Why do you ásk?'

'He was shot dead last night.'

Brenda's face lost its colour and her eyes blinked

rapidly. She turned away from him and returned her attention to her horse. Arlen reached out and grasped her arm. She was trembling, and he saw that her eyes were filled with tears. He shook her gently.

'Did your father tell you to come and lie to me?' he asked.

She nodded miserably and produced a handkerchief to wipe her eyes. 'I don't know what is going on around here, but I'm sure my father is in some kind of trouble. I don't like to go against his wishes, but I fear that his life is in danger.'

'The trouble won't go away if he doesn't face up to it,' Arlen said. 'Why don't you tell me what you do know? I'll see if there's anything I can do to help you before I leave town. When I do go you won't find much help around here, and I suspect, with those nightriders in the background, that your father has more trouble than he can handle.'

'Dad's family bought the ranch from a man named Frome. I remember that much.'

'Frome?' Arlen was startled but kept surprise out of his tone. 'That's interesting.' He nodded. 'Now let's talk about Rufus Sandor. What can you tell me about him?'

'He's from Dad's past. He turned up in town about a month ago, but didn't come near us. It was about then that Jake Pearson began to act differently. He'd been working for us about two months by then. I noticed the change in his manner because it was so against what he had seemed to be. He shouted angrily at Dad several times when he thought they were alone, and I questioned Dad after I heard Pearson bad-mouthing him.'

'Your father is due to see Sandor at the hotel in town on Saturday evening, according to the message those two men gave you,' Arlen mused. 'Everything seems to be revolving around Rufus Sandor. I'd like to know what line of work he's in at present. What was your father's job before he took over the ranch?'

'He doesn't talk much about his early years, but I think he was in the cattle business.' She paused and studied Arlen's face. 'You've met Sandor. What kind of a man is he?'

'I think he's not nice to know.'

'What could he and my dad possibly have in common?'

'I wish I had the time to find out.' Arlen grimaced.

'Are you leaving soon?'

'I'm waiting for a wire from my boss, but I think I'll have to set out for Dodge City quite soon.'

'What do you think I should do?' She looked at him helplessly, and Arlen heaved a sigh.

'I can't advise you in case things go wrong, and I shan't be around to back you if that happens. I'd like to have a chat with your father, but on the other hand I need to remain in town. I have a prisoner to consider, and there's some kind of play going on around here that I should keep an eye on. If I could be in two places at once I might have a chance of calling the right shots, but as it is, someone could be killed if I get it wrong.'

'I'd better go back to the ranch and have another talk with Dad. He's always had an open mind, and listens to my suggestions and judges them fairly, but in this case – this business with Sandor – he's like a closed book. I can't get through to him, and he won't listen to me at all.'

'If he won't talk about his past then he's probably got something to hide. You'll just have to wait until he decides to take you into his confidence. I hope he's got a clean sheet, for your sake.'

She nodded and turned to saddle her horse. Arlen watched her, trying to reach a decision. He wanted to ride with her and try to get to the bottom of this apparent mystery. He considered the situation existing in town, and told himself that most of it did not concern him. His prisoner was in jail; the stolen money safely in the bank. He could spare a few hours of this day to try and help her, and he came to a decision as she finishing saddling.

'I'll ride with you,' he said as she began to lead her horse to the door. 'Wait until I've thrown the saddle on my horse.'

She nodded, and relief showed in her face.

'I'll wait outside,' she said, and led her horse out of the barn.

Arlen saddled up and led the animal outside. Brenda swung into her saddle. He glanced along the street as he mounted. The town seemed quiet, brooding, as if waiting for something to happen. He shook his head and followed Brenda as she spurred her horse and left the town at a run. He followed her closely and they headed for the Bar F ranch.

Arlen's thoughts flitted across the broad aspects of the situation as they followed the trail. He believed that he could spend a few hours trying to sort out Buck Farrell's troubles, but realized there was little he could do if Farrell spurned his help. They rode mostly in silence. Brenda was lost in her own thoughts, and the expression on her face gave an indication of her worries.

When they came in sight of the ranch Brenda spurred her horse. She was hunched in her saddle and did not look left or right as she pounded along the trail. Arlen was watching his surroundings closely, mainly from force of habit, and he pushed his horse into a faster pace when he spotted several riders approaching the spread from high ground to the rear of the house, dropping down a slope like moving shadows.

He attracted Brenda's attention as he rode in beside her, and pointed to the riders.

'Can you identify any of them?' he demanded.

Brenda gazed at the riders until they passed out of sight behind the house. Her face had paled, and she looked at Arlen in shock.

'The leading rider looked like Jake Pearson,' she said worriedly. 'What's he doing coming back, and who are those men with him?'

'My best guess is that they are those nightriders who have been troubling you, and they're obviously up to no good. Why don't you drop back?'

She shook her head, and, as she pushed her horse to further effort, the heavy sounds of shooting erupted on the ranch and flung a string of echoes across the range. Brenda uttered a cry and spurred her horse unmercifully. Arlen cursed under his breath and rode fast to catch her, trying to grasp and restrain her, but she eluded him, and went racing into the front yard of the ranch with Arlen just behind.

As she reined up in front of the porch, two riders appeared from around the front corner to her left. Both were holding drawn guns. Arlen yelled a warning as Brenda dismounted. He drew his pistol quickly, for the newcomers were levelling their weapons.

The nearer of the two men fired and gunsmoke flared. Brenda was half out of her saddle, stepping down behind her horse. Arlen heard the crack of a bullet as it passed through the space the girl had just vacated, and his lips pulled back from his teeth as he fired. His .45 jerked in his hand. The rider who had fired was hurled back by the impact of the slug, but managed to kick his feet out of the stirrups as he lost balance. He fell heavily in the yard and remained motionless.

The second rider reined in, levelling his gun. Arlen fired again; he saw dust spurt from the man's shirt. The pistol slipped out of his hands. The violent motion of the animal as it wheeled away caused him to fall. Arlen cocked his gun. He glanced at Brenda, cowering ashen-faced and trembling behind her horse, and was concerned for her safety.

'Get back in your saddle and ride out of here.' He spoke sharply. 'Hide yourself in cover until the shooting is over.'

Brenda was so frightened she climbed into her saddle and sent the horse back across the yard. Arlen dismounted quickly and trailed his reins. The two men who had appeared from around the corner were both lying inert on the ground beside the porch. Arlen could hear a single gun shooting steadily at the back of the house, throwing hollow echoes across the range. Then several guns cut loose in a thunderous volley.

Arlen moved to the left-hand front corner of the house.

He took time to check the two fallen men. One was dead, the other unconscious, bleeding from a chest wound. Arlen removed their guns, then went along the side of the house to the rear corner. He could see several horses standing just inside the big open doorway of the barn to the rear. He eased forward slightly and saw gunsmoke rising up from three positions in the back yard. Hats and heads showed momentarily as the attackers rose up to fire. A single rifle was replying from the rear of the house.

Jake Pearson was the nearest of the three men, and Arlen recognized him instantly. He watched as Pearson tossed three slugs into the back of the house before ducking out of sight to reload. Arlen lifted his pistol and fired when Pearson exposed himself to continue shooting. The bullet hit Pearson in the side of the head and he went down with blood spurting from his wound. Arlen took on the remaining two men, and when they realized that another gun was firing at them they began to withdraw.

One man sprang up and ran towards the barn. The other, thinking he was being deserted, got up and ran also, turning to continue shooting on the run at the rear of the house. Arlen lifted his pistol and shot the nearer man in the back. When he turned his gun on the last man he could only clip the barn door as the figure ran inside. Moments later, as gun echoes began to fade, the rapid hoofbeats of a departing horse sounded at the back of the barn. Arlen heaved a sigh of relief and reloaded his gun. He looked around and saw Brenda coming along the side of the house towards him. He waved his hand, warning her to go back, but she kept coming and he returned his attention to the back yard.

'Hello the house,' he called. 'Buck Farrell, can you hear me?'

'I hear you,' Farrell replied harshly.

'I'm Jeff Arlen. Brenda is here with me. Can we come in?'

'Sure thing! There were five of them out there. Where are they now?'

'Down in the dust.' Arlen grimaced as he spoke. He could see inert bodies on the ground. Jake Pearson was lying on his back with the toes of his boots pointing up at the sky. Blood showed darkly on his head. The sound of dying echoes growled sullenly in the background.

Arlen grasped Brenda's arm. She seemed incapable of moving. Her eyes were filled with shock and her lips quivered as she gazed at the dead men. He half-supported her as they approached the kitchen door. Buck Farrell opened the door and emerged into the sun light. He was carrying a rifle. His face was grim.

'Jake Pearson was leading four riders down from the ridge back there,' Farrell said. His eyes were filled with excitement, as if he had relished the furious action.

'Pearson is dead, and so are the others, I figure. I always shoot to kill when the chips are down.' Arlen thumbed his Stetson back off his sweating forehead. 'Brenda told me you said there was no trouble out here.'

'I owe you thanks for showing up when you were needed,' Farrell said. 'I guess I made a mistake, huh?'

'So long as you put the situation to rights before it gets worse,' Arlen replied. 'I know it's none of my business, but just what is going on?'

'It's to do with what happened in my past.' Farrell

shook his head. He was sweating, but his hands were steady as he checked the Winchester. 'I guess I know what I've got to do to settle matters.'

'Rufus Sandor?' Brenda asked. She shook her head. 'You're not so young any more, Dad. And what happened in your youth to bring a pack of wolves howling on to your range?'

Farrell sighed heavily and shook his head. 'I don't wanta tell you that,' he grated.

'Is it so bad?'

'It's got worse over the years because I didn't want you to find out about it.'

'I'm gonna have to know about it now,' she replied calmly. 'You might have saved everyone a lot of trouble by being open about your past. So what were you in the old days? You did say you were in the cattle business. Does that mean you were a rustler? Were you a lawbreaker back then?'

'Don't ask questions,' Farrell snapped. 'I'll see Sandor on Saturday, and that will put an end to it.'

'It might put an end to you,' Brenda said sharply.

She looked at Arlen. Her face was creased with emotion, her eyes swimming with tears.

'Can you talk some sense into him?' she pleaded. 'He can't go up against Sandor and that outfit. If the two men who accosted me are a sample of Sandor's men then he won't have a chance of surviving.'

'Why don't you make us some coffee?' Farrell suggested. 'I'll hitch up the buckboard, load the bodies in it, run them into town and dump them on the law department.'

'Maybe you should wait a spell and give me a chance to get back to town and learn something of Sandor's plans,' Arlen said.

'I don't need any help,' Farrell retorted.

'Like you didn't need any when we rode in,' Brenda countered.

'How long was Jake Pearson working for you?' Arlen asked.

'About three months.' Farrell shook his head. 'He sure took me in. But I hadn't heard that Sandor was around at that time.'

'If he was tied in with Sandor then so were the nightriders,' Arlen mused.

'That's the way I've got it figured.' Farrell nodded.

Arlen suppressed a sigh. He moved impatiently. 'I guess I'd better start back to town,' he said. 'I've got a lot to do around there. I don't think you'll have any more trouble right now. If you're heading into town then perhaps you'd better stay there for a few days, just to see how things pan out.'

'Thanks again for your help.' Buck Farrell stuck out his hand and Arlen shook it briefly. 'We'll maybe see you in town.'

Brenda followed Arlen around the house to where they had left their horses. He swung into his saddle and took up the reins.

'I can't thank you enough,' Brenda said.

'I'm glad I was able to help.' Arlen grimaced as he met her gaze. 'You'd better be very careful after this. I won't always be around to help.'

'I'll look for you in town later,' she said, stepping back.

Arlen lifted his hand to the brim of his Stetson in farewell and swung his horse around. He rode across the yard without looking back and picked out the trail to town, riding at a fast clip. He did not relax until he had put a ridge between himself and the ranch, and as he crossed the skyline he saw a rider sitting his horse on the trail just below. He hauled on his reins. As his horse halted he recognized the rider as Elk Mitchell. The big deputy was holding a pistol in his right hand, and had a grin on his thick lips.

'I've been waiting for you, Arlen,' he said in a hoarse voice. 'Get your hands up. I'm arresting you for the murder of Squint Cullen.'

SIX

Arlen stared at Mitchell in surprise. He looked at the rock-steady pistol in the deputy's big hand and then studied the man's implacable expression. Mitchell's eyes were alive with malicious glee, and Arlen realized that he was standing on the brink of hell. Mitchell was fired-up for action.

'You know I didn't kill Cullen,' Arlen said, 'and if I did it would have been self-defence. Frome and Cullen ambushed me, and they started the shooting.'

'We're not talking about what happened.' Mitchell shook his head. 'What I'm after is the receipt you got from the bank for depositing that stolen dough; and this is the best way of getting it.'

'So you're a cheap crook!' Arlen nodded. 'I guessed as much the minute I set eyes on you. But the laugh is on you, Elk. I didn't bring the receipt out of the bank. I had a feeling something like this might happen so I had it put in an envelope and addressed to my head office in Chicago. It went out on yesterday's midnight express, and is well on its way by now. At any rate, it's beyond your grasp.'

Mitchell considered for a moment, then shrugged. 'I guess we can get by without the dough,' he said, 'but what happens to you is the same whether we get the money or not. You're going underground. I'm taking you to a cut-bank; I'll shoot you, stick you under the overhang, and drop it down on you. Then there will be one less long-nose on the scene.'

'Are those Floren's orders or did you work that out for yourself?'

'Cut the cackle. You sound like an old hen. Get rid of your guns, and don't try anything. I'll shoot you like I would a mad dog.'

Arlen discarded his pistol and rifle. He watched Mitchell intently, ready to take advantage of any lapse in his alertness. But Mitchell was well versed in handling prisoners, and his concentration did not flag. The muzzle of his pistol gaped at Arlen like a black eye.

'Let's get moving.' Mitchell waggled his gun. 'I need to get back to town in a hurry, so the sooner I finish you off the better.'

'Don't hurry on my account,' Arlen replied. 'Where are we heading?'

'Off to the right. There's bad country out that way, and I know just the spot for you.' Mitchell chuckled. 'You won't be lonesome. I've planted three bodies there in the last six months, and likely you won't be the last. Big things are gonna happen around here.'

'Which is why Rufus Sandor is in the county,' Arlen mused.

'How'd you reckon that? Sandor ain't got no part in this business.' Mitchell paused as a thought struck him. 'Or has Floren done a deal on the side? He's been playing his cards close to his vest since Sandor showed up, and I wouldn't put it past him to pull a fast one. How come you know so much about what's going on? Has Floren said something to you?'

'He's taking you for a sucker, Elk. If you trust him you'll be under a cut-bank before this is finished. But if you play it smart you could come out of this business the winner.'

'What in hell are you talking about?' Mitchell growled. 'Get moving when you're told. I ain't got all day.'

Arlen shook his reins and Mitchell moved in behind him as they proceeded. They rode south-west, heading out to the badlands, where cattle ranches were few. The ground grew rugged, broken by dry washes and gullies, littered with rock and scrub. Arlen watched for a chance to overpower Mitchell but the deputy knew his job and did not stray within reach. Arlen began to grow concerned about the situation. If he did not make an attempt to get the better of his captor then his chances of surviving were non-existent. He kept turning his head slightly for a glimpse of Mitchell, but the deputy was cute.

When they approached a ravine that had been carved in soft rock by gushing water millions of years before, Mitchell called to Arlen.

'OK, you can climb off that hoss right here. This is as far as you go.'

Arlen slid out of his saddle and looked into the mouth of the ravine, which sloped gently into the rising ground of a broken ridge. Rocks littered the ancient watercourse, and some fifty yards in there was an elbow where tumbling water had under-scored the right-hand wall to a depth of three feet. Arlen suppressed a shiver as he gazed at what looked like being his last resting place.

Mitchell dismounted and trailed his reins. He slapped the rump of Arlen's horse to move it. The startled animal reared on its hind legs instead of running, then lost its balance on the sloping ground and almost fell upon Mitchell, who yelled and hurled himself to one side. The hoofs of the horse narrowly missed Mitchell, but the animal's left fetlock gave way as the hoof hit the ground, and Mitchell scampered aside on his hands and knees to avoid the falling horse, dropping his pistol as he hurled himself clear.

When Arlen saw the incident he sprang forward, skirting his horse. He reached Mitchell as the deputy got to his feet. Arlen kicked desperately with his right foot and his leather toe thudded against Mitchell's jaw. Mitchell cursed, fell flat, rolled desperately, and scrambled up immediately, like a startled mountain lion. He paused to look around for his pistol and Arlen launched a desperate attack. His hands balled into fists and he punched Mitchell on the jaw with two swinging blows.

Mitchell was built like a young giant, and the blows seemed to have no effect on him. He did not even falter in his movements. He thrust out his open left hand and pushed Arlen away to give himself room. Arlen took the hand in his face and went backwards off balance. His right heel caught on a rock and he sprawled on his back. Mitchel dived headlong at him. Arlen saw him coming and rolled aside. Mitchell hit the ground heavily, his face striking a rock, but he jumped up with blood dripping from a cut on his chin.

Mitchell growled in his throat and hurled himself forward. His big hands were clenched and he raised them almost shoulder high as he attacked Arlen. A right-hand haymaker skimmed Arlen's chin and his knees almost gave way. Arlen gave ground, and then paused and kicked out at Mitchell's left knee. Mitchel went down, and his right hand dropped squarely on his discarded gun. He snatched up the weapon. Arlen stepped in, aimed a kick at Mitchell's gun hand, and heaved a sigh of relief when the pistol flew through the air to drop into the dust several yards away.

As Mitchell regained his feet, Arlen jumped in, lowered his head, and butted him in the stomach. He heard Mitchell's breath being expelled in a huge gasping groan. Arlen was aware that he was no match for Mitchell in a slugging fight, and he changed his tactics instinctively. He hammered blows into Mitchell's stomach and the big man retreated. Arlen lunged forward and jumped in with both feet raised. His boots thudded into Mitchell's stomach and the big man went down like a bear falling out of a tree.

Arlen crowded in, kicking Mitchell's body. Mitchell rolled, and Arlen stayed with him, his boots thudding solidly. He caught Mitchell with a powerful kick to the head, and for a moment the deputy lay motionless, breathing heavily. Arlen looked around for the discarded gun, saw it gleaming against a rock, and dived for it. He was relieved when his hand closed around the butt, and he rolled to bring the weapon into line with Mitchell's body. But the crooked deputy was already bearing down on him, and his right boot swung in for a savage kick. His dusty toe connected with Arlen's forehead. Arlen slumped instantly.

He felt no pain as the lights went out.

Sight and sound faded and Arlen struggled to retain consciousness. Flashing lights tormented his brain. Pain flared inside his skull. He gasped for air, breathed deeply, and recovered his senses. He opened his eyes to find Mitchell standing over him with the pistol levelled in his hand, the muzzle gaping at him.

'Stay down,' Mitchell commanded. 'You'll live a little longer if you do. You reckoned you could beat me, huh? Well, you ain't man enough to do that so you better give in and admit you're the loser. It's over. Now we'll get on with the chore in hand. I want you dead and buried, and the sooner the better.'

Arlen heaved a long sigh. He sat up and put his hands to his head, pressing fingers against his temples until the world stopped spinning.

'On your feet now,' Mitchell commanded. 'I'll show you where I'm gonna leave you. It's a nice quiet place.'

Arlen got to his feet. He staggered a few steps, then his balance returned and he straightened his shoulders. Mitchell was standing back well out of arm's length, his gun rock steady in his hand, and now there was a different expression on his face, a mixture of anticipation and callousness. Here was a man who liked killing and got a thrill from doing it, Arlen thought, and his small well of optimism began to dry up. So this was how his life was to end! The thought flashed through his mind like a shooting star.

'Walk into the ravine,' Mitchell said. 'It's forty yards in on the right. You can't miss it. Halt when you reach the under-cut and we'll soon put you away. Now get moving.'

Arlen glanced around at the deserted range. A couple

of buzzards were floating aimlessly in the bright blue sky, and Arlen shivered as he imagined their beaks and talons tearing lumps of flesh off his bones. He entered the ravine, his feet swishing in the fine sand, and braced himself for one last desperate attempt to get the better of the murderous deputy.

Mitchell laughed hoarsely, his voice echoing slightly in the close confines of the ravine. 'It's no use you looking around,' he observed. 'You've come to the end of your trail, so get moving. It'll soon be over.'

Arlen followed the dried-out watercourse. He walked round a slight bend and came upon a much sharper elbow, where the right-hand bank had been under-scored over the centuries when water had flowed regularly in a younger world. A deep cut had been gouged in the sandstone bank, and there were signs where stretches of the bank had been dropped to fill parts of the gap. The fillings were about six feet long, and Arlen realized that he was not the first of Mitchell's victims to visit this lonely spot.

'If you know any prayers you better say them now.' Mitchell laughed as if he had made a joke. 'Your time is getting mighty short.'

Arlen turned slowly and looked into Mitchell's face. He could see no pity or mercy in the eyes staring at him. The big deputy was enjoying this situation.

'Get down on your belly and wriggle into the gap,' Mitchell said. 'You can lie face down or on your back. It's all the same to me. I'll put a slug through your head when you're settled, and then drop the bank on you. That sandstone looks mighty hard but it crumbles real easy. Go on; get down there.'

Arlen realized that he had come to the end of his trail. He would go down fighting, but there was no chance he could get the better of Mitchell. The big deputy was waiting for him to make a last desperate attempt, and the steady pistol pointing at him was ready to slam a bullet into him. He drew a deep breath and restrained it, summoning up all his reserves of strength and energy. He had been in many tight corners in his tough career but this was the worst. The knowledge did not deter him. He had nothing to lose.

'I can read your mind, Arlen,' said Mitchell tauntingly. 'You're gonna jump me and die trying to best me. OK, so get to it. I'm ready.'

'What about the ten thousand dollars?' Arlen demanded. 'I'll do a deal with you – my life for the money. We can ride into town right now and I'll pick up the dough for you. You've got me beat, and I'll do anything to save my life.'

Mitchell waggled his gun. 'No deal. I would have agreed if you'd made the offer when I first got the drop on you, but now you've wasted a lot of my time.'

Mitchell raised the pistol and took aim at Arlen's chest. Arlen clenched his teeth, deciding to dive low at the deputy. He drew a deep breath, but before he could launch an attack he heard the smack of a bullet striking flesh and saw Mitchell jump and twist. The echoing crash of a rifle shot blasted through the tense silence as Mitchell's gun spilled out of his hands and he fell in a twitching heap.

Arlen jumped forward and snatched up the pistol. He spun round, his eyes wide, shock spreading through him.

He saw Brenda Farrell standing twenty yards down the ravine, a rifle in her hands and gunsmoke drifting above her head. The girl's face was ashen and she was trembling. Arlen bent over Mitchel to check him, discovered that he was still alive with a bullet hole in his lower left ribs, and then hurried to Brenda's side.

'Is he dead?' Brenda asked faintly. She looked as if she were about to collapse, and Arlen slid an arm around her waist to support her.

'He's still breathing.' He drew a deep breath. There was a pounding in his ears and his heart thudded rapidly. 'You saved my life, Brenda. Mitchell was about to shoot me and bury me under that cut-bank. How'd you manage to turn up at the right moment?'

'After you left the ranch my dad decided I should ride back to town, and urged me to catch up with you for protection. I saw you riding over the ridge near to the house, and when I reached that spot I saw Mitchell holding a gun on you. I arrived as you threw down your guns, and when Mitchell made you ride with him I collected your guns and followed. What got into Mitchell? I saw what he planned to do, and shot him when it looked like he was going to pull the trigger on you.'

'I've never been closer to death.' Arlen took his weapons from her, holstered the pistol, and went back to Mitchell, who was stirring. Arlen examined Mitchell's bullet wound more closely. 'It looks like you live, Mitchell,' he observed. 'I'm gonna take you to town and put you behind bars.'

'Who shot me?' Mitchell lifted his head and saw Brenda standing near by, hands to her face. 'I knew I should have done something about her weeks ago,' he said with a groan.

'Now it's too late for you,' Arlen said. 'Do you wanta tell me what's going on around here?'

'Go to hell,' Mitchell replied.

Arlen fetched Mitchell's horse. He motioned for Brenda to take his rifle again, and the girl suppressed a shudder as she did so.

'Keep him covered,' Arlen told her. 'Shoot him if he tries anything. I've got to get him into his saddle. He's going back to town, and then I'll find out what's going on around here.'

Brenda cocked the rifle and took aim at Mitchell.

'Get up, Mitchell.' Arlen said.

'The hell I can!' Mitchell groaned. 'She put that bullet through my ribs.'

'If it's as bad as you think then you'll die before I can get you back to town. You better make the effort. The alternative is to lie here and cash in. I don't give a damn what you decide, but make up your mind quick.'

Mitchell lay motionless for some moments, then rolled on to his left side. He thrust his hands against the ground and got to his hands and knees, where he paused, head hanging. He was groaning and cursing. Arlen had no intention of helping him. He waited, and suddenly Mitchell was lumbering to his feet like a bear awakening from hibernation. He lurched forward and grabbed his saddle horn, hung there for some moments, then made the effort to get into his saddle. After two attempts he managed to get his left foot into a stirrup, and almost pulled the horse off balance when he lunged upwards into leather.

He slumped in the saddle, found his other stirrup, and clung to the saddle horn. Arlen took the reins and led the horse to where his mount was standing. He swung into his saddle, tied Mitchell's reins to his saddle horn, and drew his pistol. Brenda hurried to her horse and sprang into the saddle, anxious to get away from the ravine. She rode in beside Arlen, and nodded when he gazed questioningly at her. She was pale and shaken, and her hands trembled as she urged her horse forward. Arlen smiled encouragingly when she met his gaze, her teeth clenched with determination.

'You're doing good, so hang in there,' he said. 'Have you got somewhere to stay in town?'

'I have friends, but I wouldn't want to take trouble to them.'

'We don't know what is going on around here,' he commented. 'Your father should have given us some idea of what happened, but he was pretty close-lipped, so we don't know what lies ahead. He seems to think you'll be safe in town. Or does he expect me to watch out for you? I'll certainly do that.'

'I won't be a burden on you,' she said quietly.

'Hey, if it wasn't for you I'd be lying under that cut-bank right now with a ton of earth on my face. You saved my life and I won't ever forget that. Mitchell told me he's planted several men in that ravine in the past six months, so I reckon he'll hang for his sins. I'm gonna take real good care of you. Don't ever think you'll be a burden on me.'

Brenda shrugged. She looked doubtful, but his words seemed to relieve her. They continued to town, and it was mid-afternoon when they sighted Sunset Ridge. Mitchell was slumped in his saddle, semi-conscious. His wound had stopped bleeding. His dry lips were moving silently.

The main street was silent and still as they rode along it to the law office. Heat was baking the dust. A dog lying in the shade under the sidewalk in front of the store lifted its head to gaze at them but was too indolent even to bark at their passing. The door of the law office was wide open, and when Arlen reined up in front of it he could see Sheriff Floren sitting at his desk, writing busily.

Floren looked up at the sound of hoofs, stared at Arlen for some moments, then caught sight of Mitchell, sitting hung over in his saddle. He sprang to his feet, overturning his chair in his haste. Arlen dismounted, listening to the sound of Floren's boots pounding the bare boards, and was facing the office door with his hand close to his holstered gun when the sheriff stuck his nose into the street.

'What happened?' Floren demanded. 'Mitchell's bleeding. Who shot him?'

'Brenda did,' Arlen spoke in a clipped tone, certain that Floren would be involved in anything his big deputy was caught up in.

Floren looked at Brenda, his face expressing surprise. He opened his mouth to question her but Arlen spoke first.

'Hold your horses, Sheriff. Listen to what I've got to say before you start in.'

Floren closed his mouth. His eyes were like broken glass, and Arlen was wondering if the sheriff had a guilty conscience.

'I'm listening,' Floren said.

Arlen explained the incident in a dry, flat tone, his eyes

never leaving the sheriff's weathered face. Floren's features seemed to turn to stone. His lips pulled into a thin, uncompromising line. When Arlen finished his narrative, Floren moved impatiently.

'We'd better put him on a bunk in a cell and I'll get the doctor to look at him,' he said stiffly. 'I was surprised this morning when he said he had a hunch he needed to check out. He left town early, but I had no idea what was on his mind.'

'He said he wanted to get his hands on the money Frome stole from the bank,' said Arlen as he helped Floren get Mitchell out of his saddle. They took him into the office and then into a cell and put him on a bunk. Arlen stepped back and watched Floren lock the cell door. He glanced at the forlorn figure of Frome, sitting hunched on his bunk in his cell, and looked around, noting that the men who had held up Brenda were no longer in their cells.

'Where are Darley and Gauvin, Sheriff?' Arlen demanded.

'I turned them loose. Brenda said they didn't try to rob her so I let them go.'

'I told you I saw one of them holding a knife to her throat. That should have been enough to put them before a judge.'

'There was nothing I could charge them with.'

'They work for Sandor. How is he involved in this business?'

'How should I know?' Floren shrugged.

'You showed a great deal of respect for Sandor last night when you searched his hotel room.'

'And now you think I'm working along with him, huh?'

'Did you know Mitchell was gonna try and kill me today?'

'If I had any idea that was on his mind I would have stuck him behind bars.' Floren glanced at Mitchell. 'Let's continue this later, huh? I need to fetch Doc Murray over to check Mitchell. You'll charge him with attempting to kill you, huh?'

'That's the least I'll do.' Arlen nodded. 'I'll come back to you later, Floren. I wanta have a talk with Sandor before I do anything else.'

'Don't bother looking for him.' A half-smile came to Floren's lips. 'He left town just after you pulled out earlier, and it looked like he is not coming back. I checked with the hotel after he left, and he's gone for good. Heck, I don't even know why he was here.'

Arlen was shocked by the news. He gazed at Floren, but the sheriff left him standing and departed to fetch the doctor to Mitchell. Arlen looked at Brenda, who was waiting patiently in the street doorway, her face showing the anguish she was feeling. Arlen sighed and went to the girl. For the first time in his life he was at a loss. But he forced himself to act normally, although his brain was racing as he tried to make sense of what was happening. A lot was going on in the background, and now that he had started an investigation he would not stop until he had uncovered the bare bones of it.

SEVEN

Brenda's face was expressionless as she gazed at Arlen. She looked pallid and shocked. Her eyes seemed dead, vacant. Arlen saw that her teeth were chattering, and he slid an arm around her shoulders.

'You've suffered a bad shock,' he observed. 'Let's go to the hotel and get you a coffee or something stronger. I need to talk to the receptionist. Floren told me that Sandor has pulled out.'

'I don't believe that,' she said firmly. She became animated, and worry filled her gaze. 'He wouldn't leave now. He hasn't settled his business with my father.'

'We'll worry about that later. Right now I want to settle you.'

'I'm sorry for being such a trouble to you.'

'Don't worry about that.' He smiled at her. 'You saved my life this morning, and I'm gonna owe you for the rest of my days.'

The bar at the hotel was deserted. Arlen sat Brenda down at a small table and went through to the kitchen, which was also deserted. There was a coffee pot on the stove and he checked it. The pot was full and hot. He poured two cups, added sugar to the one intended for Brenda, and went back to the bar.

'You can have something stronger if you fancy it,' he suggested.

Brenda smiled and shook her head. 'My father would skin me if I touched anything stronger than coffee,' she replied.

The hot sweet coffee put a tinge of colour in her cheeks. She became more animated and began to take notice of her surroundings.

'Do you really think Sandor has gone for good?' she asked.

'I wouldn't want to make a guess. I'll ask around, and then do some checking. But I can't accept that he would leave so abruptly, unless he has finished whatever business brought him here in the first place. Obviously something bad happened between him and your father years ago, and Sandor seemed a pretty determined man. I'd like to see your father turn up here in town and stay put until the trouble has been settled. Now I want to see you safely with your friends so I can attend to my own business.'

They walked into hotel lobby. The clerk, Hollins, was behind the desk, and Arlen approached him. Hollins's face bore the bruises around the left eye that he had collected from the sheriff. He looked at Arlen with glaring animosity.

'I hear that Rufus Sandor has departed,' Arlen said. 'Has he gone for good or will he return?' He paused, and when Hollins opened his mouth to reply he said quickly, 'Don't give me the old story that you can't talk about hotel guests.' He reached into an inside pocket of his jacket and produced his deputy US marshal badge. 'Just answer the question, huh?'

Hollins closed his mouth and compressed his lips. He seemed disinclined to answer, but then thought better of his intention and forced a smile.

'Mr Sandor told me he had some urgent business in Kansas City and left in a hurry, saying he wouldn't be back.'

Arlen nodded. 'Have you any idea what business interested him around here? He was in town about three weeks, I understand.'

'He didn't talk business in my hearing. In fact he was close-mouthed in everything. He didn't even pass the time of day.'

'I was in his room with him this morning when someone outside put some shots through the window up there,' Arlen observed. 'Perhaps that scared him off.'

'Mr Sandor did not seem to be the type to scare easily.' Hollins smiled.

Arlen went back to where Brenda was standing by the door. She was looking across the street. He held her arm and led her out to the sidewalk. She did not seem to have any interest in her surroundings.

'It looks like Sandor has gone for good,' he told her, 'but I wouldn't trust him.' Arlen checked the street before leaving the cover of the hotel. 'Where does your friend live?'

'I won't stay there,' Brenda replied. 'It might bring trouble down on them. I'll put up at the guest house next to the bank. Mrs Parnell is a motherly woman and keeps a fine place.'

'I'll see you settled before I do my own job,' he said. 'I've got things to handle around town this morning so I'll look you up this afternoon. Your father should be here by then, and we'll have another talk with him.'

Brenda led the way along the street to a large house with a wide garden. A tall, thin woman was hanging out washing; she paused and came to the gate when Brenda called her. In a matter of moments Brenda was led into the house; she paused in the doorway and lifted a hand in acknowledgement to Arlen. He nodded and turned away, his expression hardening as he went back to the law office.

Floren was seated at his desk. He got to his feet and picked up the bunch of keys lying on a corner of the desk.

'Doc Murray says Mitchell will survive, so the sooner you give me your statement about what happened this morning the sooner I can get things moving. You'll have to stick around until Mitchell's trial, so you could help me run the law around here until then.'

'You don't have any trouble around here worth talking about,' Arlen responded. 'Sandor has gone and won't be back. Mitchell won't come to trial for a couple of months, I guess, so I can take Frome to Dodge City and be back here before anything happens. If Mitchell pleads guilty then you won't need me anyway.'

'You might change your mind when you hear what Mitchell has got to say. He tried to do a deal with me but I turned him down. You can get him to talk about what's on his mind if you offer him a deal – his liberty in return for information about Sandor.'

'What's he got to do with Sandor?' Arlen demanded.

He followed Floren into the cells. Mitchell was lying on

his bunk, his shirt opened to the waist, his chest bound tightly in bandages. He was breathing laboriously; his eyes were closed, his face pale. Arlen glanced into the cell where Frome was sitting on his bunk. There was an expression of hopelessness on Frome's face, and Arlen shook his head as he considered the situation.

Mitchell opened his eyes when Floren unlocked the door of his cell. He gazed up at Arlen, groaned, and then closed his eyes again.

'I don't feel like talking right now,' he said.

'You can wear him down,' Floren suggested. 'I'll leave you here in the office. I'd better ride out to Farrell's place and get the lowdown on what happened out there.'

'I'll hold the fort until you get back,' Arlen agreed. 'I need to talk to Frome some more and get a statement from him, and Mitchell will tell me what's on his mind before I've done with him.'

Floren handed the cell keys to Arlen and departed quickly. Arlen stood beside Mitchell's bunk.

'So you wanta do a deal,' he said as an opener. 'What have you got to deal with?'

'Plenty.' Mitchell did not open his eyes. He stifled a groan as he moved slightly, and sweat broke out in tiny beads on his forehead.

'OK, I'm listening. Spill the beans.'

'Not so fast. How do I know you'll keep your end of any deal we make?'

'You'll just have to trust me. So what's on your mind? Tell me why you wanted to kill me this morning. I have nothing to do with any trouble around here. I didn't threaten you in any way. In a day or so I'll be leaving with my prisoner and you won't ever see me again. So why did you attack me?'

'I was paid to do it.' Mitchell opened his eyes and grinned.

'How much, and who paid you?'

'Rufus Sandor gave me a couple of hundred bucks to bury you.'

'Why?'

'Hell if I know! He didn't say and I didn't ask. All I was interested in was the dough.'

'So you're a cold-blooded killer as well as being a crooked deputy, huh? I had you figured like that the minute I set eyes on you. So what's new? Sandor has left town now, and the word is that he's not coming back.'

'I can tell you he's mighty interested in Brenda Farrell, so maybe he doesn't like you hanging around her.'

'What was Sandor doing around here anyway?'

'He said business, and left it at that. So what about doing a deal?'

'You ain't got anything to deal with,' Arlen said. 'You haven't told me anything that I don't already know. Have you got anything else?'

'If you wanta leave this town alive then you'll do a deal.' Mitchell stifled a groan as he tried to find a more comfortable position on the bunk.

'You've already made it clear that I've got some problems. So what's new?'

'Floren is tied in with Sandor.'

'I already figured that out. You're holding a poor hand, Mitchell. The best thing you can do is throw it in. You're a loser.'

Mitchell closed his eyes and remained motionless. Arlen left the cell and locked the door. He went to Frome's cell and studied him for several moments. Frome looked up and then averted his gaze.

'I want a statement from you, Frome, telling me why you stole the money and if anyone else is involved in the crime. When I've settled my side of the business we can head back to Dodge.'

'I've got nothing to say.' Frome spoke in a low tone. 'You've got the money back so let it go at that. How long do you think I'll get in prison?'

'I'd say a minimum of five years. You worked in that bank and abused your position of trust. They'll make an example of you for letting the system down. You should have known better. Why did you head for this town? Have you got kinfolk around here?'

Frome did not answer, and Arlen lost his patience and went into the front office.

He sat at the sheriff's desk, found a blank piece of paper, and scribbled a few notes. Then he sat thinking over the situation, and realized that he would have to push Buck Farrell a bit harder to learn something. Most of this trouble seemed to stem from what had happened between Farrell and Sandor years before. His impatience increased and he picked up the bunch of keys, left the office, and locked the door behind him.

Arlen walked to the telegraph office. He was hoping for a reply to the wire he had sent to his head office, but there was nothing for him, and his impatience increased. He looked around the street. The town seemed dead this morning, and he wondered if it was because Sandor had

107

departed. He walked to the livery barn, and Joe Henty stepped out of a stall when he heard Arlen's boots on the hard-packed ground.

'I was wondering when I would see you again,' Henty said.

'My horse is outside the law office, and Brenda Farrell's too,' Arlen said. 'Fetch them in and feed and water them, will you? I'm tied in with the local law for a couple of days.'

'I'll do anything for you,' Henty said. 'That's why I've been waiting to see you. Sandor pulled out this morning, but he left two men behind, and I heard him giving them their orders. They're a couple of killers; Darley and Gauvin. You had them jailed for attacking Brenda. Floren turned them loose, and now they're waiting for you. Their orders are to kill you and kidnap Brenda. I walked past the law office earlier, hoping to see you because I won't talk to Floren. You've found a lot of trouble today, huh?'

Arlen tensed. 'Thanks, old-timer,' he rapped, and dashed out of the stable. He ran along the sidewalk to Mrs Parnell's guest house, his gaze checking out every likely ambush spot he came across. The town was silent and still, as if waiting for something to happen. He was breathless when he reached the house, and he paused for a moment to recover. He leaned a hand on the gatepost, his chest heaving, and at that moment, he heard Brenda cry out. He dashed into the house, caught a glimpse of a man standing on the stairs about halfway up. He saw a gun in the man's hand swing towards him, and recognized Darley as he hurled himself to one side.

He reached for his gun instinctively; it came into his hand like a well-trained dog. He dropped to one knee as

Darley turned swiftly to take him on, and the gunman became unbalanced, almost fell down the stairs, He reached out with his left hand to grab a rail, and when his attention turned fully upon Arlen he discovered that he was staring into the muzzle of Arlen's gun.

'Drop it,' Arlen rapped.

Darley paused. His gun was pointing at the stair beneath his feet. Arlen could see he was trying to decide what to do, and when Darley jerked his muzzle upward Arlen squeezed his trigger and tossed a slug into the right side of his chest. The crash of the shot thundered through the house. Darley dropped his gun and lifted both hands to his chest. He leaned forward from the waist and pitched headlong down the stairs, to land in a twitching heap at Arlen's feet.

Arlen mounted the stairs two at a time. As he reached the upper landing a gun blasted from the rear of the house. The bullet passed through Arlen's left arm above the elbow like a flash of lightning, then splintered the handrail at his left elbow. A man was standing in the doorway of a bedroom along the landing. He ducked back into the room as Arlen levelled his pistol. A door slammed. Brenda cried out again, the sound coming from the room the man had entered. Arlen tiptoed along the landing. He ignored the pain in his right arm, but was dimly aware that blood was flowing from his wound.

He raised his right leg as he reached the door and kicked at the centre panel. The door splintered and flew open. Arlen lurched into the room, gun hand extended. The room was deserted. The window was wide open and he ran to it. There was a fire escape outside that led down into the back garden. A gun crashed and glass shattered above his head. He ducked but remained in the opening, looking for Gauvin. He saw the man running away through a stand of trees, dragging Brenda along with him.

Three horses were standing in the background, their reins trailing. Arlen turned and ran to the stairs. As he started to descend he saw Darley hunched on the bottom stair, a Colt .45 wavering in his right hand. Arlen did not hesitate. He clattered down two more stairs, then launched himself feet first at Darley. His boots thudded into the gunman and Darley slumped without a sound. Arlen jumped over the motionless figure. His legs gave way and he fell heavily.

His head struck a wall, but he did not lose consciousness, and struggled to get up. He saw his gun on the bottom stair and could not remember dropping it. He snatched it up, saw a figure close by out of a corner of his eye, and turned his gun. It was Mrs Parnell, gazing at him with terror in her expression. He lowered his gun and sat down on the bottom stair. He holstered his gun and gripped the bullet wound in his left arm with the fingers of his right hand.

'Fetch the doctor,' he said. Mrs Parnell turned and ran out of the house.

The doctor seemed a long time arriving, but suddenly he was standing in front of Arlen, a tall, smartly dressed man wearing a blue town suit and carrying a leather bag.

'I'm Doc Murray. Who are you?'

'Jeff Arlen, private detective, and deputy US marshal.'

Doc Murray nodded and opened his bag. He produced scissors and cut Arlen's left sleeve open to the shoulder.

Arlen bore his ministrations stoically. His wound soon stopped bleeding, and the doc bandaged the upper arm.

'I'll put the arm in a sling,' Murray said, 'and you'll have to avoid using it if possible. The bone wasn't touched by the bullet so there's a good chance the wound will heal without complications.'

'Thanks, Doc.' Arlen pushed himself to his feet. For a moment he was dizzy, but made an effort to overcome his weakness and looked at Mrs Parnell, who was leaning against the front door, gasping for breath. Her face was chalky white and she seemed to be on the point of collapse. Arlen took hold of her arm, led her into a room, and seated her on a chair.

'Where is Brenda?' Mrs Parnell gasped.

'There were two men after her,' Arlen replied. 'The one who went upstairs after her took her down the fire escape at the rear window and they rode off together. Tell Sheriff Floren what happened, will you? I'm going to fetch Brenda back.'

He turned to the doctor, who was examining Darley.

'Is he still alive, Doc?' he demanded.

'He's breathing, and I think he'll make it.'

Arlen dropped the cell keys beside the doctor's medical bag. 'If he's still alive when you've finished with him, then put him behind bars. I'll be back later to sort out any problems.'

He left the house by the back door and crossed the rear garden to where Darley's horse was standing with trailing reins. The animal backed away nervously when he approached it but he caught the reins and held them while he checked for horse tracks. He saw where two horses had departed, checked the general direction they were taking, and mounted to ride in pursuit.

The tracks led him out of town, but out of sight of the buildings they veered left and began to circle until they were heading in the opposite direction. Arlen pushed the horse along at a fast clip, his gaze intent on the tracks because they were his only link with Brenda. His left arm ached intolerably from shoulder to wrist, and the wound itself was throbbing. He pulled the brim of his Stetson lower over his eyes and pushed on, his reflexes honed, his right hand ready to pull his gun and start shooting. He was worried about the girl and could not understand why she had been taken.

It did not take him long to realize that Gauvin was taking Brenda in the direction of the Farrell ranch. He wondered about the situation behind the shooting, but his mind was set on catching up with Gauvin and freeing Brenda. When he crossed a flat stretch of range he saw two riders ahead in the distance. He quickened his pace but Gauvin was urging his horse along at a near gallop, forcing Brenda to stay with him, and Arlen could make little impression on the gap between them.

He rode with more caution, hoping to close the gap without being seen. When he saw the Bar F ranch in the distance he eased to his right and found cover in screening trees. He remained among the trees, watching Gauvin ride into the ranch yard. A man appeared in the doorway of the ranch house, and Arlen frowned when he recognized Rufus Sandor. There was no sign of Buck Farrell. Sandor escorted Brenda into the house while Gauvin returned to his saddle and came back along the tracks he had left.

Arlen realized that he must have been spotted and rode away instantly. He did not desire contact with any of Sandor's gang until he had checked out the ranch and learned what the situation was. He spurred the horse and crossed a ridge before Gauvin appeared on his back trail. With cover between him and Gauvin he angled to his right and rode hard for more cover. When he was satisfied that he had cleared the area he slowed his retreat, dismounted in tree cover, and waited to see if Gauvin would reappear.

Minutes later Gauvin showed on a crest on Arlen's back trail; he spent some minutes surveying the deserted range, then turned and rode to Arlen's right. He eventually left the skyline and did not show again. Arlen heaved a sigh of relief and dismounted. He trailed his reins and sat down to lean his back against the trunk of a tree, his mind roving over the problems facing him. He needed to learn what the trouble was between Buck Farrell and Rufus Sandor, and until he did so he could do nothing constructive.

While the horse took a breather Arlen tilted his Stetson over his eyes and tried to rest, but his wound would not permit relaxation. Then he became aware of the faint smell of cigarette smoke irritating his nostrils. He turned his head to face the breeze. As he did so he became aware of a figure rising up out of the undergrowth some yards away, and of a double-barrelled shotgun that was covering him with deadly twin eyes.

EIGHT

Arlen resisted the impulse to reach for his pistol. He lifted his hands clear of his waist, then became aware that he was being confronted by Buck Farrell. The rancher recognized Arlen at the same time and lowered the shotgun.

'What in hell are you doing here, Arlen?'

'I'm asking you the same question,' Arlen replied.

'I told Brenda to catch up with you on the trail to town, and to stay away from the ranch until the trouble is over.'

'You saved my life when you did that, but I ain't got time to talk about it now. I took Brenda into town like you wanted, and two of Sandor's men grabbed her. I downed one of them but the other got clear with her. They rode into your ranch, and Sandor was waiting there like he owned the place. So what gives, huh? Why is Sandor on your spread while you're skulking out here?'

'Trouble has caught up with me,' Farrell said heavily. 'I always guessed it would, but I ignored the signs, and now I've lost out. I only got clear of the spread when Sandor and his outfit rode in. I was ready to shoot it out with him until it hit me that I'd be making a bad mistake by killing him.'

'You're talking in riddles.' Arlen shook his head. 'The time for keeping your mouth shut is long gone. Didn't you hear me say that Sandor has got his hands on Brenda? There's no telling what he might do.'

'That's been his aim for years – to get her away from me. Now he's done it, and I ought to get the hell out and leave the gal in peace.'

'It would be easier for you to tell me what this is all about rather than let me make wild guesses. Brenda saved my life this morning, and I'm ready to return the compliment if she's in trouble.'

'Sandor will kill you if you don't clear out now.' Farrell swung around when a twig cracked sharply somewhere behind him. He levelled his shotgun as he peered around. 'Did you hear that?' he demanded. 'Someone is prowling around.'

Arlen got to his feet and drew his pistol. He moved forward to Farrell's shoulder, his eyes narrowed to slits as he checked his surroundings. He caught a glimpse of two horses moving at a walk from left to right just outside the tree line. The riders were hunched in their saddles. Sunlight glinted on drawn weapons. A twig snapped to Arlen's right and he turned in the direction of the sound, to see Gauvin limping forward on foot, a pistol in his hand. Two more steps would bring him into the open from the surrounding trees. Arlen cocked his gun, and Gauvin paused, his head turning quickly to locate the metallic sound.

Farrell dropped to one knee. Arlen remained upright,

ready to fight. Gauvin came on again. Arlen levelled his gun. Gauvin cleared the trees and came face to face with Arlen. There was a gap of ten yards between them. Gauvin stopped as if he had walked into the side of a barn. Surprise showed in his face, as if he had not really expected to find anyone. Then he swung his pistol to cover Arlen, who squeezed his trigger finger. The crash of the shot was over-loud beneath the trees. The slug struck Gauvin in the right shoulder and he staggered backwards. His pistol fired a single shot; the bullet struck the ground between his feet. He fell and lay inert on his face in the undergrowth.

The echoes of the shot fled through bright space, fading slowly into the distance.

'Hey, Gauvin,' a rider called sharply. 'What you doing in there? Have you found Farrell? Is he dead? Sandor said to kill him on sight.'

Farrell sprang to his feet at the sound of the voice and thumbed back the hammers of his shotgun. He moved forward to the outer fringe of the trees until he could see the two riders, now sitting their horses, guns levelled at the tree line. Farrell jerked the butt of the long gun into his right shoulder, squinted along the barrels and fired all in one movement. A horse screamed as half a load of whirling buckshot slammed into it. The rider took the other half of the deadly pellets and tumbled out of the saddle. The horse went down with threshing hoofs. Arlen winced at the sight, and swung his pistol to cover the second rider. But the man was already heading for elsewhere, hunched over in his saddle and moving fast.

The heavy detonation seemed to hang in the air. Farrell

was frozen in a hunched-over position, gripping the shotgun, his shoulders heaving with the power of his breathing.

'You didn't have to use that scattergun,' Arlen reproved.

'You heard what was said.' Farrell spoke jerkily, as if he had no control over his voice. 'Sandor said to kill me.'

'Let's get out of here.' Arlen glanced around. 'Get your horse and follow me. We'll head to town.'

'We'll never make it.' Farrell sounded as if he had lost his nerve. But he went to his horse and swung into the saddle.

Arlen fetched his horse and mounted. He rode clear of the trees and Farrell followed him. A bullet crackled between them, and Farrell's horse jumped nervously. While Farrell was fighting to control the animal, Arlen slid his Winchester from his saddle boot and jacked a shell into the breech. He saw gunsmoke drifting from a ridge forty yards to the right, and then spotted a Stetson easing up above the skyline. He aimed quickly, fired, and the hat disappeared instantly.

The next moment three riders appeared on the ridge and started shooting with six-guns, throwing lead carelessly, intent on overwhelming their opposition. Arlen returned fire, and after his first shot one of the riders fell out of his saddle. The other two rode back beyond the ridge and disappeared from sight. Arlen heard a thump and when he looked round he saw Farrell lying on the ground. He cursed, dismounted, hurried to the rancher's side and dropped to one knee beside him.

Farrell was lying on his face. Blood stained his left side.

Arlen glanced around before turning Farrell on to his back. Farrell's eyes were flickering but did not open. Arlen saw by the growing bloodstain that the rancher had been struck high in the chest, and he opened Farrell's shirt to reveal a neat round bullet hole in the upper chest. He lifted Farrell into a sitting position and examined his back There was no blood, which indicated that the bullet had not passed through the body, and that was not so good. The wound needed immediate attention.

Arlen looked around for trouble but there were no signs of the men who had been attacking them. He went to his horse and opened a saddle-bag. He always carried some rough bandaging; just in case the worst happened. Quickly he plugged Farrell's wound and placed a bandage over it. Farrell regained his senses as Arlen finished his ministrations, and he looked up at Arlen, his eyes dull with shock.

'You're OK,' Arlen said. 'You stopped a slug but it doesn't look too bad. Those gunnies seem to have had enough for now so we'll make our way to town and get the doc to look you over. Do you feel like making the ride?'

Farrell nodded, and Arlen helped him to his feet, boosted him into his saddle, and stuck the reins into his hands. He fetched his horse and mounted, sided Farrell, and they headed out at a canter. The silence surrounding them was a blessing, and Arlen remained alert as he took his bearings and headed back to Sunset Ridge.

He was concerned about Brenda Farrell, but he did not think Sandor would harm her; at that moment Buck Farrell's needs were much greater than his daughter's. They continued to town without trouble and reached it

118

during late afternoon. Farrell was slumped deep in his saddle, his hands pressed against his saddle horn to maintain his balance. His face was ashen. Blood stained his vest and shirt. Arlen sighed with relief when he reined up outside the doctor's house, but jumped from his saddle when Farrell began to slip sideways out of leather. He caught hold of the rancher and eased him to the sidewalk. Farrell lay as though dead, and Arlen hurried to the doctor's door to summon help.

Doc Murray took one look at Farrell and motioned for Arlen to take hold of the rancher's feet. They carried Farrell into the house and placed him on the examination table in the medical office.

'Do what you can for Farrell,' Arlen said. 'I'll be over at the law office. I'll hold Farrell in there when you've fixed him up.'

'Is he under arrest?'

Arlen shook his head. 'No. I'm taking him in for his own protection.'

Arlen left the house. He led the two horses across the street to the jail and hitched them to a rail. The office door was ajar and he entered cautiously, his hand close to the butt of his holstered gun. He expected to see Floren; there was no sign of the sheriff but the bunch of cell keys was on a corner of the desk. Arlen picked them up and went into the cell block. He was slightly surprised to find both Frome and Mitchell still in their cells. Mitchell was asleep but Frome was seated on the foot of his bunk, staring moodily at the floor and looking as if he had not moved in the last two hours.

Arlen stepped up to Frome's door. 'What's happened

around here while I've been away?' he demanded.

'How would I know?' Frome countered. 'I ain't seen anyone.'

'Has the sheriff been back?'

'Not to my knowledge.'

Arlen gave in to his impatience. He left the office and climbed into his saddle. He could not rest while Brenda was out at the ranch with Sandor. He rode back along the street and headed for the Farrell spread, steeling himself for the action that awaited him there. The sun was low on the skyline when he eventually reined in on a rise overlooking the ranch.

There was no activity around the spread as night closed in. Several horses were in the corral, and a solitary lamp was alight in a bedroom, shining like a welcoming beacon through the gathering shadows. Arlen dismounted and dropped to the ground. He was close to exhaustion. The wound in his left arm was painful but did not trouble him unduly. He checked his pistol. He was ready for action, and waited out the final minutes to full darkness.

A cooling breeze blew steadily into his face as he watched the last of the red-gold sunset die out of the sky over Sunset Ridge. There was a tang of pines in his nostrils and his eyes watered. The thin line of gold that clung to the sky in the west suddenly winked and vanished like a ghost of the day. Full darkness held sway for long moments, then stars began to shine.

Arlen got to his feet, patted his horse, and started down a slope towards the cow spread. He was unemotional as he walked steadily towards the one light burning in the house. His rifle was in his left hand and he kept his right hand close to the butt of his holstered gun. A tense silence surrounded him as he moved through the night. Far out in the blackness of the night the haunting wail of a preying coyote sounded through the stillness. He suppressed a sigh and slid between two bars of the fence around the yard.

The dark mass of the bunkhouse was barely visible at ground level; the roof showed where it was silhouetted against the sky. There was no yellow lamp glow in the low building. Arlen turned his attention to the ranch house.

He avoided the hard pan of the yard and circled until he reached the cover of the barn, where a pig was grunting in its sty inside. He was about to move on when he caught the smell of cigarette smoke and saw a red glow inside the wide doorway of the barn. He froze instantly, scarcely breathing. A man coughed, then there was the clink of metal against the door. Arlen eased back behind the front corner of the building. He drew his pistol and held it ready. The time for action had arrived.

He eased around the corner and walked slowly to the door of the barn, which was three-quarters open. He stayed close to the front wall and eased in behind the door. A boot scraped inside the barn and he tried to pinpoint the exact position of the guard. The next moment the man emerged from the interior, almost taking Arlen by surprise. The man paused, a gasp escaping him. Arlen recovered quickly and swung his pistol in a tight arc. The barrel slammed against the man's left temple and he fell away into the shadows.

Arlen went after him and bent to administer another blow. The man groaned and relaxed. Arlen dragged him back into the barn. He used the man's neckerchief to tie his hands behind his back, and then secured his legs with his gunbelt, buckling it tightly round the ankles before dragging him deeper into the barn.

A thin crescent of the moon showed itself just above the ridge, and silvery light gave a ghostly appearance to the ranch. Arlen stood in the doorway of the barn and looked around. He went forward across the space to the back of the house and paused by the kitchen door; tried it and found it locked. Turning, he went to a shadowed rear corner and moved slowly to the front of the house. He was still some yards from the front corner when he heard the front door slam; he dropped to one knee in the shadows, his gun ready. Voices sounded and two men came off the side of the porch. They paused by the corner.

'So you know what to do, Harvey,' one said. 'Sandor gave the word that the detective, Arlen, must be put out of it. You can get the sheriff or his deputy to handle the chore, but if they won't do it then you handle it yourself. Have you got that? If you make a mess of it then don't show your face around here again. Your second job is to find Buck Farrell and kill him. Get moving, and do it right.'

'You can leave it to me,' Harvey replied. 'I'll head for town right now. But what are you gonna do while I'm gone?'

'I'm heading out to Beaver Creek shortly to bring in the rest of the gang.'

The pair separated. One went to the corral to saddle up; the other returned to the house. Arlen got to his feet. He heaved a sigh as he wished he could be in two places at the same time. He thought of Brenda, and wondered why Sandor had kidnapped her. When he considered Buck Farrell, wounded and alone in town, with a gunman setting out to murder him, Arlen knew what he had to do next.

He walked openly across to the corral. Harvey was throwing a saddle across the back of a horse. He turned at the sound of Arlen's boots on the hard ground.

'Is there something else?' he demanded.

'Yeah.' Arlen lunged forward over the last few feet and clubbed the man with his pistol.

Harvey collapsed without a sound. Arlen bent and fumbled around the fallen saddle. He found a coiled rope and used it to hogtie the man. When he had finished he straightened and looked around. The ranch was silent, and he wondered how long he could get away with fighting a one-man war.

He dragged the man out of the corral and deposited him behind the bunkhouse. His wounded left arm was aching badly as he returned to the house. But he had to get to Brenda before heading back to town.

The moonlight had strengthened and now the ranch lay bathed in a silvery glow that pinpointed every movement. Arlen reached the front corner of the house and stepped on to the porch. Lamplight was streaming out of a front window, and he needed to risk a look through the window in order to locate Brenda. The silence surrounding him was so intense that he could hear the creaking of the house as it cooled after the heat of the day. He drew a deep breath and moved forward.

He felt exposed as he stepped into the lamplight streaming through the window and looked quickly into the big room. Brenda was seated in a leather chair in a corner. Her expression was harsh, and she kept glancing at the porch door as if trying to steel herself to make a run for it. Two gun men were in the room. One was seated at a wooden table, reading a newspaper, the other was seated opposite Brenda, talking incessantly to her although she was apparently ignoring him.

Arlen stepped quickly into the surrounding shadows and placed his back to the front wall of the house. His keen gaze took in the yard and he sighed with relief when he saw no movement out there. He moved to the door, cocked his pistol and went into action, pushing open the door and stepping quickly into the big room. He was across the threshold before either man was aware of his presence. The man at the table made a belated move, coming to his feet and reaching for his gun, but he stayed his hand when he saw that he had no chance of beating Arlen. The other man looked over his shoulder at Arlen, then raised his hands slowly.

'That's good,' Arlen said quietly. 'Where's Sandor?'

'He ain't here,' said the man at the table. 'He rode out just after they brought the girl in.'

'Where's he gone?'

'You'll have to ask him,' said the second man. 'We don't know his plans.'

'Get rid of your guns,' Arlen commanded. 'One at a time, and you at the table can start. Do it slow, and toss your weapons into that corner over there.'

Both men obeyed without hesitation.

'Down on your faces,' Arlen said, handing Brenda a discarded gun. 'Shoot them dead if they do more than blink,' he told her. Brenda took the pistol and cocked it.

Arlen saw a coiled rope hanging from a peg in a corner and fetched it. He holstered his pistol and bound both men tightly. As he straightened, the porch door opened noisily and two men entered the room. Arlen swung to face them, reaching for his gun. He was close to the door and the nearer man reached out and struck him on the jaw with a powerful blow of his clenched right hand. Arlen staggered back a couple of steps, shaking his head; his gun, clearing leather, slipped from his hand and thudded on the floor.

The second newcomer drew his pistol quickly. Arlen heard the sound of it being cocked. The man who had hit him came forward with his hands up defensively. A shot was fired, and Arlen was too busy defending himself to see what happened. He ducked a vicious right and delivered a blow with his own right, catching the man on the side of the jaw. He stepped forward a short pace and kicked viciously. The toe of his right foot thudded into the man's groin and sent him to the floor in a sprawling heap.

Arlen turned quickly, looking towards Brenda, the sound of the shot ringing in his ears. He saw the girl near the fireplace, both hands on the gun he had given her; a wisp of smoke was curling up from the muzzle. He saw the second man on the floor with blood spurting from a wound in his left shoulder. Arlen sighed with relief, gave Brenda a grateful nod, and disarmed the men. Neither was fatally wounded, and he set to work, binding them with the rest of the rope.

He moved to the door and dropped the bar into place. Only then did he relax.

'That's the second time today you've saved my life,' he said huskily. 'It's beginning to be a habit. What's been happening here? I saw Gauvin bring you in, and Sandor was on the porch. What did he say to you?'

'He told me to wait in the house until he could find the time to talk to me.'

'So you still don't know what is going on?' He saw her shake her head, and explained to her about her father. Her face took on an even paler shade of white. 'He's OK,' he added quickly. 'I left him with the doctor and came straight back here to get you. Now we'd better get out of here before anyone else pops out the woodpile. I'm wondering where Sandor has gone, and why he came here in the first place. He's given orders for your father to be killed, and also put out the word on me. I've been fighting back, but it looks like Sandor won't stop until he's collected a slug.'

He led the way out of the house and headed for the corral; he saddled Brenda's horse and collected his own mount when they were ready to leave. The ranch was silent now. Arlen swung into his saddle and they rode out. As they cleared the spread he hoped that they were finished with the gun trouble.

NINE

Arlen watched their surroundings closely on the trail back to town and was relieved when they reached the back of the livery barn without incident. They attended to the needs of their mounts, then Arlen led Brenda along the back lots into an alley beside the jail. The town seemed unduly quiet but he drew his pistol as they left the alley and went to the law office. Arlen opened the door and peered inside. A man in shirtsleeves was seated at the desk, wearing a law star on his chest. Arlen ushered Brenda inside and closed the door.

The man got to his feet and came forward, his expression filled with curiosity. He was tall and thin, middle-aged, and wore a gunbelt around his waist. His blue eyes gleamed as he confronted Arlen.

'I've been expecting you to show up,' he said. 'I'm Pete Woodrow, and I've been called in as a temporary law man because Sheriff Floren has disappeared.'

'Disappeared?' Arlen frowned.

'He hasn't been seen since he rode out of town this morning around noon. No one knows where he is, and he took his things from the room he rents in town. It looks like he's gone for good.'

'I wonder why.' Arlen thought he knew why. Floren was no fool. With Mitchell exposed as a would-be killer, Floren must have realized that he would be next to come under suspicion.

Woodrow glanced at Brenda. 'I'm glad to see you're unharmed,' he observed. 'I've got Buck in a cell. The doc said to put him behind bars for his own protection.'

'How is my father, Mr Woodrow?' Brenda demanded.

'Don't worry about him,' Woodrow replied.

'Is his life in danger?' Brenda persisted.

'He's sitting up, taking notice, and quite happy to remain where he is. Doc says he'll be OK in a couple of weeks. Have you come from the ranch? Who was it out there shooting at your pa?'

'We don't know yet what the trouble is,' Arlen cut in. 'I think it would be a good idea for us to talk to Buck and hear what he's got to say about the shooting.'

'I'm told you're a deputy US marshal.' Woodrow eyed Arlen speculatively. 'Will you be taking over here?'

'No. I'm involved, and I'll stay to see this trouble out, but otherwise I'm just helping the local law.'

Woodrow picked up the cell keys and held them out to Arlen. 'I'll leave you to question Buck,' he said. 'He didn't have anything to say when I talked to him earlier.'

Arlen took the keys and ushered Brenda into the cell block. Buck Farrell was in an end cell with the door open. Brenda ran into the cell and bent over her father. Arlen looked at Elk Mitchell, who was drowsing on the bunk in his cell, then stepped close to the door of Frome's cell.

The bank robber gazed at him, his face expressionless, his eyes dull. Arlen went into the end cell behind Brenda and looked down at Farrell.

The rancher was pale-faced: shocked by the wound he had received. His shoulder was heavily bandaged. He was conscious and looked up at Arlen as Brenda embraced and kissed him.

'What is going on, Dad?' Brenda cried. 'Why is Sandor on the ranch? Why are his men trying to kill you? You can't remain silent any longer. You've got to tell us what is happening. Who is Rufus Sandor and why is he after your blood?'

She sat down on the bunk and held her father's hand. Farrell kept his eyes on Arlen.

'Thank you for saving my life,' he said huskily. 'If you hadn't showed up I would be dead now. Sandor took me by surprise when he came to the ranch with his gang, and I was shocked when some of them followed me when I made a run for it. I was on my last legs when you showed up.'

'I was only returning a favour,' Arlen said smoothly. 'Brenda saved my life this morning. That big skunk Mitchell had me cold when Brenda shot him. But that's all water down the creek. What I need to know now is why Sandor is after you. Are you gonna explain what's been going on? If we don't put a stop to him then the next time he makes a try for you I might not be around.'

Farrell nodded. His forehead was beaded with sweat. 'I agree. I'll tell you what's been going on. Rufus Sandor and Alec Frome are half-brothers. They had different fathers but the same mother. Chuck Sandor, Rufus's father, married my mother, and brought Rufus and Alec to the ranch when I was a boy. Chuck was killed later by a posse hunting rustlers. My mother reared Rufus and Alec until they were old enough to leave the ranch. Rufus took after his father and went into rustling; Alec left for Kansas and took up banking.'

'So what happened to bring Rufus back to your ranch?' asked Arlen.

'He decided that rustling was getting too hot for him and planned to take over my spread. His father put some money into the ranch before he was killed, and Rufus reckoned he was entitled to take what he could get. The trouble built up when he began to put pressure on me. I turned to the local law for help but they had thrown in with Sandor. When you turned up on Frome's trail you forced Sandor's hand; and now he's taken over my ranch.'

'He can't get away with that,' Arlen answered. 'Floren and Mitchell have been shown up for what they are, and a new sheriff will be honest. You'll get your spread back with no trouble at all.'

'You don't know Sandor.' Farrell shook his head. 'He was planning to kidnap Brenda and hold her as a lever to put pressure on me. I didn't think he would go down that trail, but now I know he'll do anything to get what he figures is owed to him.'

'He might change his mind about that when he learns what happened out at your place when I rode in,' Arlen observed. 'But I heard he's got more men at Beaver Creek, and he's sending for them to make his final play.'

'At Beaver Creek?' Farrell nodded slowly. 'There's a derelict horse ranch out there. So that's where Sandor's hiding his gang. If a posse could drop on them now they wouldn't have a chance, and Sandor's power would be wiped out. I wish I could sit a horse.'

'I'll do what I can,' Arlen said grimly. 'Where is Beaver Creek?'

'It's about ten miles west of my place.' Farrell grimaced as he added, 'But with no law to talk of in town, there's not much hope of getting a posse together. Sandor is gonna ride roughshod over us and we won't have a chance.'

'I ain't been doing too badly against him,' Arlen mused. 'I ain't heard from my boss yet so I've still got some time to play with. Sandor's gang have shot at me and I reckon I owe them something for that. Who do I see about turning out a posse?'

'John Larrabee, the blacksmith, is a staunch man of the law.' Farrell brightened. 'He rides out with every posse. Talk to him and he'll get some men together.'

Arlen glanced around the jail and shook his head. 'I can't leave this pace unguarded. If Sandor dropped in here while I'm away he'd undo everything I've accomplished.'

'Larrabee can handle a posse better than any sheriff,' Farrell opined. 'Give him a free hand with a dozen men and he'll get the job done.'

'I'll talk to Larrabee. And there's a new law man in the office because Floren has upped stakes and pulled out. If we can get an extra couple of men in, then there should be no problem.' Arlen glanced at Brenda. 'I reckon you should stay put in here until we get this business cleaned up,' he suggested. 'Sandor would like to get his hands on you again.'

'I wouldn't set foot outside the door even if the place

was on fire,' she replied. 'I'll stay here and keep an eye on my dad.'

Arlen went back into the front office. Woodrow was seated at the desk. Arlen told him what was needed and Woodrow departed to find some dependable men. Arlen sat down to reflect on what had to be done. He had an edge for as long as Sandor was unaware of the situation in town, and a posse on the way to Beaver Creek would put the rustler at a big disadvantage.

Impatience began to seep into Arlen. He was a man of quick action, and regarded inactivity as time wasted. He checked his gun and refilled its empty chambers. When Woodrow came back into the office Arlen got to his feet.

'I'd better see Larrabee about taking a posse out to Beaver Creek,' he said.

'I've talked to Larrabee and he's getting a posse together. He'll be riding out with a dozen men inside thirty minutes. There'll be two extra men in here shortly. You don't have to worry, Marshal. This is a lawful town and the men in it will do you proud. It'll all be taken care of.'

'I wish I had your confidence.' Arlen shook his head. 'It's my experience that when things look like turning out right is when the unexpected happens, and I shan't be happy until Sandor is in jail. I'll take a turn around town and see that Larrabee gets away. But I've a mind to ride with the posse. Do you think you can hold this place until I get back?'

'If we're hit by trouble then we can fort up in here,' Woodrow said confidently. 'The place is built to withstand a siege, and any shooting would bring a dozen armed men running.'

'I'll take your word for it.' Arlen nodded. 'I'll go with the posse. Get your men in here quick as you can and lock everything down tight.'

He went to the door and glanced around the street. The afternoon was wearing away. There were signs that a posse was gathering, and he went along the sidewalk to the saloon, where horses were being tethered outside. A big, muscular man in shirtsleeves was standing by the batwings. He was loaded for bear, with a pistol belted around his waist and a rifle in his left hand. There was eagerness on his bearded face. He was filled with impatience, and it showed.

'Are you Larrabee?' Arlen asked.

'Sure thing,' the blacksmith replied. 'Who are you?'

'Jeff Arlen, deputy US marshal. There's a gang of rustlers out at Beaver Creek, run by a man called Rufus Sandor.'

'Glad to know you, Marshal.' Larrabee stuck out his right hand, and his grip was like iron when Arlen shook it. 'I've seen Sandor around town, and he looked like a bad 'un to me. We'll soon take care of him and his gang.'

'I'm thinking of riding with you,' Arlen said, 'but you will lead the posse. I want to make sure we get all of the bad men. But I've got a sneaking feeling that I ought to remain here in town, just in case.'

'We're riding in ten minutes,' Larrabee said. 'The stragglers are beginning to show up. I can handle the posse if you wanta remain here.'

Arlen nodded, his decision made. 'Ride to Beaver Creek by way of the Farrell spread,' he suggested. 'There was shooting out there earlier and there might be some cleaning up to do. If the rustlers are coming this way at all they'll probably make for the ranch first.'

'Consider it done.' Larrabee grinned. 'We'll be gone all night. If you conceal yourself somewhere around town you might find some rats sneaking out of cover when the posse pulls out.'

'That is in my mind,' Arlen replied. He entered the saloon, ordered a beer, and sat down at a small table to drink it.

The posse rode out twenty minutes later, and Arlen, standing inside the batwings of the saloon, watched them depart. The town seemed as dead as Boot Hill after the sound of receding hoofs had faded into silence. Arlen looked around the dusty street from his point of vantage. He saw some loafers in front of the general store, no doubt talking about the posse riding out, but mainly the street was quiet, with little movement. He craned forward to check the alleys, and saw nothing to alarm him.

His thoughts meandered across the situation, and he wondered why Alec Frome had headed back this way after robbing the bank where he had worked for twenty years. Had Frome returned to Sunset Ridge to meet up with Sandor? A stream of questions welled up in Arlen's questing mind. Filled with a sense of disquiet he heaved a sigh and left the saloon to head for the law office, aware that he needed answers from Frome to fill some of the gaps bothering him.

The door of the law office was locked, and Arlen knocked. Woodrow opened the door, a pistol in his right hand. His face was taut, his eyes narrowed, but he relaxed and smiled when he saw Arlen.

'Everything is OK here, Marshal,' he reported. 'I've got a couple of good men coming in who will back me, and I'm happy with the set-up.'

'The posse is on its way to Beaver Creek,' Arlen said. 'I reckon Larrabee can handle the chore, and I really need to be around here, just in case. I want to question my prisoner, Frome.'

'You know where to find him.' Woodrow grinned. 'My two men will be along in a few moments. They're getting cartridges from the general store. We'll have food delivered to us at mealtimes from the diner. Everything is taken care of.'

Arlen picked up the bunch of cell keys from the desk and went into the cell block. He saw Brenda sitting with her father in the unlocked cell and lifted a hand to her. She smiled wanly, but seemed much happier, so he went to stand at the door of Frome's cell. Frome looked up at him, his face expressionless, eyes dull and body listless.

Arlen said: 'I know about you and Sandor. Did you know he was around here?'

'I've got nothing to say,' Frome shook his head, his eyes studying the floor.

'That means you arranged with him to meet here,' Arlen said.

'I didn't say that,' Frome snapped.

Arlen grinned. 'I don't believe in coincidence. Is that why you stole the dough from the bank? You didn't want to come here empty handed. But I spoiled the deal for you. You've got nothing from your exploit, and you're facing several years in prison for your pains. No wonder you're looking sick. And Sandor will leave you sitting behind bars. But you might be able to help yourself by telling me what's going on. I'll see that the judge hears of any help you can give me, and that will go down in your favour. So stop sitting there looking like a man who's shot himself in the foot and start talking.'

Frome shook his head and turned away. He stretched out on his bunk and faced the bars. Arlen watched him for some moments before turning his attention to Elk Mitchell, who was awake and gazing at him with malice in his expression.

'How are you doing, Mitchell?' Arlen demanded. 'Are you ready to talk about your problems? You made a big mistake trying to kill me. No doubt you expected to be turned loose by Floren the minute my back was turned, but the joke is on you. Floren has got out of the game. You're on your own now, with no hole card, and you'll be an old man by the time you finish the prison sentence that's coming your way.'

'Try telling me something I don't know,' Mitchell rasped. 'But this game ain't done yet, not by a long rope, and you won't be standing on top of the pile when the end comes. You'll be crowing like a rooster when they shoot you in the back.'

'Did you know Floren was gonna run out on you?' Arlen demanded.

'If you think that then you better think again.' Mitchell sneered. 'The game is too big for anyone to up stakes before it's finished. Why do you think I tried to kill you? There's rich pickings around here, and I'll get my share when you're dead.'

'Marshal,' Buck Farrell called. 'I reckon Mitchell is

talking about the bank being robbed. I heard Sandor talking to one of his men out at the ranch. I didn't catch all of it, but the bank was mentioned, and so was Floren. I reckon you should have a word with the banker and put him on his guard.'

Arlen nodded. He left the cells and entered the front office. As he threw the bunch of keys on the desk someone hammered on the street door. Woodrow walked over to it.

'Hold it,' Arlen called. 'Don't open the door yet. Ask who's out there.'

Woodrow nodded and moved closer to the door. 'Who is it,' he demanded.

'It's Pete Dormer,' came the reply. 'I've got food for the prisoners and guards. Why's the door locked?'

'We're expecting trouble, Pete, so the door stays locked,' Woodrow replied.

'Who is Dormer?' Arlen demanded.

'He works at the diner along the street. I saw him earlier and told him to bring grub along at meal times.'

'Let him in.' Arlen drew his pistol and cocked it. 'Stand to one side when you open the door. Let's see who's out there.'

Woodrow put a key in the big lock, turned it, jerked open the door and moved quickly to one side. As the door swung wide three men holding guns lunged forward in a rush to enter the office. Woodrow lifted his pistol but the foremost intruder slammed a gun in his face and he dropped instantly. Arlen, standing six feet from the door, lifted his pistol, his finger trembling on the trigger. He saw a gun being levelled at him and started shooting.

The quick blast of gunfire was heavy and furious. Gun

smoke flew. Arlen's first shot took the leading man in the shoulder and he went down in a stumble, ramming his face into the floor. Arlen dropped to one knee as the other two started shooting. He ducked as slugs snarled around him. He triggered two more shots as his pistol swung to cover each of the men, and he was too fast for them. Both went down and remained motionless. Arlen drew a quick breath and cocked his gun, but the shooting was over.

He got to his feet and went forward to collect discarded guns. The echoes of the shooting rolled across the town as if in a hurry to be gone.

Woodrow got up, staggered, then bent to pick up his gun. There was blood on his face. Arlen stepped over the motionless men and went out to the sidewalk. He looked around, ready for more trouble, but the street was deserted. He holstered his gun, and dragged the wounded men in through the doorway. Woodrow slammed the door and relocked it.

'So what have we got here?' Arlen demanded.

'That's Pete Dormer,' Woodrow said, indicating the man who had hit him. He looked at the other two men and shook his head. 'They're strangers to me,' he added.

'I've seen both of them before,' Arlen said. 'They ride with Sandor. I saw them out at Farrell's ranch. So what's Dormer doing with two of Sandor's men? And he sure didn't bring any grub with him.'

He examined the men. All three were bleeding. Dormer was unconscious but the other two were conscious and groaning in pain.

'Fetch the doctor,' Arlen said. 'I'll cover the office until you get back.'

Woodrow hurried out and Arlen stood in the doorway watching the street, his gun in his hand. Brenda called to him and he turned to see her standing in the doorway to the cells.

'It's OK,' he said. 'Go back into the cells and remain there.'

She looked at the fallen men and turned away hurriedly. Arlen heaved a sigh. The trouble was not over yet, not by a long rope. He tried to assess the situation, but did not possess sufficient knowledge of local affairs to assess what was going on. He wondered about Floren and tried to guess at Sandor's next move. The fact that an attack had been made on the jail indicated that Sandor was interested in his half-brother Alec Frome.

Woodrow returned, accompanied by Doc Murray, and the injured men were treated and placed in cells. Arlen confronted Dormer, a tall, thin, stick of a man in his fifties. Dormer was in great pain. His teeth were clenched, his lips bloodless.

'You're in a lot of trouble, Dormer,' Arlen commented. 'What's a townsman with a decent job doing attacking the local jail with outlaws?'

'I didn't do it from choice,' Dormer replied. 'These bad men have been in town several weeks. They frequented the diner and made friends with me. I knew they were bad men, and turned them down when they suggested I should come to the jail with them to gain admittance. They know the diner supplies prisoners with food, and reckoned you'd open the door to me. But they said my wife would suffer if I didn't help them out so I came along.'

'The two men who came with you work for Sandor,' Arlen said. 'What do you know about him?'

'I've seen him around town but had nothing to do with him.'

'What was supposed to happen if you got into the jail?'

'They were gonna bust Alec Frome out and take him out of town. They said no one would get hurt.'

'So they lied to you. You made a big mistake, Dormer.'

'There was nothing else I could do,' Dormer said sorrowfully. 'They used my wife as a lever against me – said they'd kill her if I didn't help them.'

Arlen went to the cell containing the other two men. One was unconscious; the other was awake, stretched out on his bunk, eyes blinking. Arlen entered the cell and looked down at the prisoner.

'What's your name?' he demanded.

'Smith.'

'You were trying to bust Frome out of jail. Where is Sandor?'

'Find him and ask him,' Smith growled.

'I'll certainly find him,' Arlen responded. 'And when I get him he'll join you in here.'

He returned to the front office to find Woodrow opening the door to the two men who were joining him to guard the jail. Woodrow introduced them as Jackson and Townley; and they looked capable.

'Be very careful from now on,' Arlen suggested to Woodrow. 'Check all callers before you open the door.'

'You can count on me doing that,' Woodrow replied. 'What are you gonna do?'

'I need to trace Sandor, and I've got a feeling that

Floren is still around.'

'He's cleared out.' Woodrow shook his head. 'You won't see him again.'

'I'm not so sure.' Arlen grimaced. 'I'll be back later.'

He left the office and stood for some moments looking around the street, seeing nothing to arouse suspicion. The town was silent and still. But he was not satisfied. He had a hunch that trouble was lurking in the background and he did not know where to look to confront it. He went along the sidewalk to the bank and entered.

As he closed the door a gun muzzle jabbed against his spine and a hand jerked his pistol from its holster. A harsh voice warned him to remain still. He glanced over his shoulder, and a pang darted through him when he found himself looking into the baleful features of the ex-sheriff, Gus Floren.

TEN

Arlen gazed into Floren's harsh face. Floren stepped back, his gun levelled. Arlen glanced around the interior of the bank. Three other men were present. One was standing at the counter, holding a gun on the teller, who was motionless with his hands raised. Another was in the doorway leading into the banker's office, gun in hand, and Roarke, the banker, was standing with his hands raised. The third man was Jethro Bain, Sandor's top gun. He was at the big safe, stuffing money into cloth bags.

'I was hoping you'd turn up, Arlen,' Floren said, grinning. 'It'll save me coming to look for you. Everything was going along OK around here until you showed up, sticking your long nose into everything. Mitchell made a mess of trying to put you away.'

'I'm sorry I spoiled your fun,' Arlen said. 'So you're working for Sandor now?'

'Yeah, from the first moment he came to town. He made me an offer I couldn't turn down.' Floren nodded. 'We're cleaning up around here before moving on.'

'I guess you arranged for the jail break a few minutes ago, huh?'

'And you stopped it!' Floren rasped. 'I heard the shooting. But Sandor will get Frome out of there when the rest of his crew show up. You sent the posse to Beaver Creek, but Sandor's gang ain't there – never have been. It's a wild goose chase for the posse, and we'll be long gone before they get back here. Now stand over there in that corner and put your hands up. We'll be leaving in a few minutes, and you'll be dead when we go. You stuck your nose into our business once too often, and it's gonna cost you your life.'

Arlen moved to the nearest corner and stood with his hands raised. Floren remained by the door, watching the street and keeping an eye on Arlen, who watched the scene with little hope of doing anything to stop the robbery: caught flat-footed. He had a two-shot derringer in his hip pocket, which he carried as a back-up weapon, but even if he could get a hand to the weapon he would need more than two shots to deal with this set-up.

He watched Bain cleaning out the safe. The gunman was intent on the piles of money, his hands quick and nervous. Arlen eased his right hand down to his chest, his movement coinciding with Floren's gaze turning elsewhere. His fingers dropped to the level of his right hip – left hand remaining in the air. Sweat broke out on his forehead but he continued his movement, aware that he had no option.

Floren's head began to turn in his direction again, but at that moment a figure appeared outside the door. The handle was turned and a man came bustling into the big room, almost colliding with Floren, who cursed and jammed the muzzle of his pistol against the newcomer's chest.

'Where in hell did you come from?' Floren demanded as the man raised his hands.

Arlen reached into his hip pocket, secured a grip on the derringer, and jerked it free. He dropped to one knee as he lifted the weapon into the aim, and squeezed the trigger, sending a .41 slug at Jethro Bain. The slug took Bain in the side above the waist, and as the shot crashed Arlen lunged out of the corner and dived at Floren, who was partly covered from him by the newcomer.

The man covering the banker jerked around, and stood motionless for a moment, paralysed by shock. Arlen reached Floren as the ex-sheriff struck the newcomer a blow to the head with the barrel of his Colt. The man collapsed against him, blocking Floren's attempt to shoot at Arlen, who crashed against the newcomer, his left hand snaking out around him to secure a grip on Floren's gun wrist.

Floren's gun exploded. The bullet missed as Arlen forced the gun hand wide. He released his hold on his derringer and grasped Floren's pistol with his right hand, jerking the big weapon out of Floren's hand. The newcomer threw his arms around Floren and wrestled him to the floor. Arlen turned Floren's pistol, grasped the butt, and moved aside a couple of steps as he transferred his attention to the man covering the banker. Out of a corner of his eye he saw Bain sprawled on the floor in front of the big safe, apparently out of it, his left leg kicking convulsively.

The man covering the banker could have shot Arlen but instead of fighting he ran into the banker's office, pushing Roarke out of his way. Arlen fired a shot but the bullet clipped the edge of the office door an instant after the man had disappeared.

Roarke leaned against the doorjamb, his legs suddenly weak. Arlen glanced at Floren and saw he was flat on his back with the newcomer holding him down. Arlen crossed to the safe and bent over Bain. Sandor's top gunman was dead; the .41 derringer slug had penetrated his ribs and slammed into his heart. Arlen went back to the door. The newcomer was getting to his feet. Floren was lying on his back, his eyes closed.

'What's going on?' the newcomer demanded. 'Is it a robbery?'

'It was, and you stopped it,' Arlen said. 'What's your name?'

'Jack Colby.'

'Go talk to the banker. He'll wanta thank you for horning in like that.'

Arlen bent over Floren, grasped his shoulder and shook him. Floren opened his eyes and glared at Arlen.

'On your feet,' Arlen rapped. 'You're gonna see the inside of the jail. Let's get moving.'

Floren arose. Roarke came forward, badly shaken. He began to thank Arlen, who cut him short.

'You'd better lock your safe,' Arlen advised. 'I think there's still a lot of trouble coming to town, and you'd better prepare for the worst.'

He pushed Floren towards the door and they departed. As they crossed the street Arlen was thinking fast. Sandor had managed to get a posse sent out to the wrong place, which hinted that he was planning to come in and take over while the posse was away.

Arlen jabbed Floren's spine with the muzzle of his pistol. 'Hurry it up,' he rasped. 'I need to get ready for Sandor's bunch.'

They reached the jail, where Arlen called out to Woodrow, who opened the door.

'Lock Floren in a cell,' Arlen said. 'I caught him robbing the bank.'

Woodrow was shocked, but said nothing. He drew his gun, picked up the cell keys, and motioned for Floren to precede him. Arlen followed them and watched until Floren was locked in a cell. He moved on to Buck Farrell's cell, and frowned when he saw that Brenda was not there.

'Where's Brenda?' Arlen demanded.

'She's gone to the store.' Woodrow shrugged. 'Said there were some things she needed. She'll be back shortly.'

'I told her to remain here for a very good reason,' Arlen said. 'Be prepared for trouble. Sandor wants Frome out of jail, and he'll have a bunch of men with him if he does show up.'

He left the office, paused until the door was barred behind him, and then went across the street to the general store. Several men were standing in a group outside the bank, attracted by the shooting. Arlen entered the store and looked around. There was no sign of Brenda, so he approached the storekeeper, who was serving a woman.

'Has Brenda Farrell been in?' Arlen asked.

'I haven't seen her today,' the storekeeper replied.

Arlen walked out to the street, his mind buzzing. He looked around, searching for a glimpse of Brenda's slim figure. Had she gone to visit her friend before visiting the store? Or had Sandor grabbed her? Suspicion filled the darker recesses of his mind. He pictured the girl's face as he went to the bank and addressed the half-dozen men standing on the sidewalk.

'Has anyone seen Brenda Farrell on the street this morning?' he asked.

Keen eyes studied his face. He waited for a reply. Most of the men shook their heads without hesitation. One man said he hadn't seen the girl in weeks.

'I saw her about ten minutes ago,' another said. 'She came out the jail and went thataway.' He pointed along the street in the direction of the shanty town. 'She's got a friend living down there – Marylou Ford – who lives in the big green cabin on the left.'

'Thanks.' Arlen strode along the street, watching for trouble. He reached the end of the street and paused to take in his surroundings. He saw a big green cabin and went across to it. A young woman was in the garden, weeding a flower bed. She looked up as Arlen's shadow fell across her.

'Marylou Ford?' he queried.

'That's me.' She was tall and slender, pretty in a home-spun way. Her brown eyes were filled with curiosity as she regarded him.

'I'm Jeff Arlen,' he told her. 'I'm looking for Brenda Farrell.'

'I didn't know Brenda was in town.' Marylou shook her head. 'I haven't seen her at all.'

Arlen partly explained the situation, and then asked: 'Is there anyone else in town she might visit?'

Marylou shook her head. 'If I see her I'll tell her you're looking for her.'

'Tell her to come back to the jail,' he replied, raising his hat as he turned away.

He returned to the law office, and was disappointed when Woodrow told him that Brenda had not returned. He went through to the cells and confronted Buck Farrell.

'Brenda seems to have disappeared,' Arlen told him. 'No one in town has seen her. Did she say anything to you before she left?'

Farrell shook his head, groaning as he shifted position. 'She just said she was going to the store. There were some things she wanted. I told her to hurry back.'

Arlen departed again, his impatience aggravated by a growing fear that Brenda had found trouble. He walked to the front of the bank, where the group of men had increased. One of the men confronted him.

'I'm Tom Dolan,' he said. 'I hear you're looking for Brenda Farrell. I was putting a couple of windows in a cabin in shanty town, and I saw Brenda going into Squint Cullen's place about half an hour ago. She didn't come out again while I was down that way, so likely she's still there. Maybe she's visiting with Squint's widow.'

'Thanks. I'll check it out.' Arlen set off along the street.

He was now worried about Brenda and his fears increased with each step he took. Why would Brenda visit a woman such as Mrs Cullen? He approached the cabin and knocked on the door. When there was no reply he peered through a window. Mrs Cullen was inside, seated at a table and reading a newspaper. He knocked on the window and she looked up at him; waved a hand, intimating that he should go, and then returned her attention to the newspaper. Arlen heaved a sigh and hammered on the window.

'Open the door, Mrs Cullen,' he called. 'I need to talk to you.'

'Go away,' she replied.

Arlen went back to the door and tried it. He discovered it was barred and threw his weight against it, but it was too solid for his efforts and barely moved. He went back to the window and knocked again.

'You'd better open the door,' he called. 'If you don't I'll throw you in jail.'

Mrs Cullen arose from the table and came to the door. She opened it fractionally and stuck her head out.

'What do you want?' she demanded. 'You killed Squint.'

'I didn't kill Squint. The man who hired him is the one who shot him.'

She began to close the door but Arlen stopped her. He pushed the door wider.

'I'm looking for Brenda Farrell,' he said.

'Who's she? I don't know her. Why do you think she's here?'

'I was told she called on you less than an hour ago.'

'Well, you were told wrong. I ain't seen a soul all day.'

Arlen looked around the big room. It was neat and clean; nothing was out of place. But his keen gaze noticed that a cushion in a big leather chair was awry and a corner of a piece of red material was sticking up. He crossed the room, pulled the cushion forward and picked up the red material. He looked at it, then turned to Mrs Cullen.

'This is a neckerchief,' he said, 'and Brenda Farrell was wearing one just like it the last time I saw her.' He buried his nose in the material and breathed deeply. 'It even smells of her perfume. So she was here. Come on, admit it. She was here, so where is she now?'

'That belongs to my daughter. She came in this morning.'

'You're lying. Listen to me and get this good, Mrs Cullen. If anything bad happens to Brenda Farrell then you'll be charged accordingly. You'd better think very carefully before you say anything more. The man who killed your husband is a brother of the man who wants to get his hands on Brenda, and I can't imagine you wanting to help either of them. So tell me what is going on. Why did Brenda come here to see you, and where is she now?'

Mrs Cullen remained silent, her eyes narrowed, her face expressionless. Her mouth was set in a thin line.

'Well?' Arlen demanded. 'You'd better speak up. I've warned you of the consequences if you don't. Brenda was here. That's obvious. Now tell me what's going on. She was seen coming in here and didn't leave. Where is she?'

'Sheriff Floren told me this morning the girl was in trouble and wanted somewhere to hide for a spell. He asked me to take her in. So if there's any problem about that then you'd better talk to him.'

'Floren is no longer the sheriff. He's behind bars right now, so he's out of it. Where's the girl? Tell me what happened here.'

'She left a few minutes before you showed up,' Mrs Cullen said reluctantly. 'I don't know where she went.'

'She didn't come here looking for shelter. She was perfectly safe in the jail. I'll give you one last chance to tell me the truth. Lie again and you'll spend a long time behind bars. Do I make myself clear?

'The girl told Floren she wanted to meet a man, and Floren asked me to take her in until that man showed up. She came this afternoon, and I kept her here until someone came to collect her. That's all I can tell you.'

Arlen studied her harsh face and decided she was telling the truth. He sighed, fighting impatience.

'What was the name of the man she wanted to see? Was it Sandor?'

'I don't know.'

'Have you any idea where she was taken?'

Mrs Cullen shook her head, and it was obvious to Arlen that he would get nothing more from her.

'I might be back to do some more checking, so make up your mind to cooperate with me. Give me any more trouble and I'll lock you up for a long time.'

He left the cabin and hurried back to the law office, impatient to confront Floren. When he walked into the cell block he looked at the ex-sheriff, saw a grin on his face and a triumphant gleam in his eyes. He crossed to the door of Floren's cell and reached through the bars to seize hold of Floren's jacket before jerking him up against the door. Floren tried unsuccessfully to break his hold.

'You've got some explaining to do, Floren,' Arlen said harshly.

'It was me who told her, Arlen.' Frome spoke from the next cell. 'I said my brother Rufus would spare her father if she did as she was told. After you arrested me, Floren agreed to help me if I gave him a share of the money I stole from the bank.'

'You don't have that money,' Arlen said. 'It's in the bank, and it'll remain there. Didn't Floren tell you he failed to rob the bank? Now I want to know where Sandor is holed up. Make up your mind to the fact that no one is going to escape from this jail. I'd like to see Sandor and his gang try to bust you out of here.' He laughed harshly. 'He's kidding you if that's what he told you. He'll know better than to try it.'

'That's why he wants Brenda,' Frome replied. 'He'll use her as a lever against you and her father to get what he wants. You'll be hearing from him mighty quick, and you don't have to be told what he wants – Floren and me out of here in exchange for Brenda.'

Arlen shook his head. 'I'll do a deal with you,' he said without hesitation. 'Tell me where Sandor is, and when I get Brenda back I'll let you go.'

'I'd rather trust Sandor than you,' Frome said. 'Turn me loose first. I'll ride with you to show you where Rufus will be, and you free me when you see Brenda out there. Floren goes with me.'

'I'll take a chance on that,' Arlen said. 'I'll take you and Floren out of here in handcuffs, and free you the minute I set eyes on Brenda, but I'll kill the pair of you if I find that you're lying. And I'll take a lawman along to back me.'

'Open the cell doors,' Floren said quickly. 'You've got a deal.'

Arlen went into the front office and picked up the cell keys. Woodrow, seated at the desk, looked up at him; he did not protest when Arlen explained what he was going to do.

'I'll go with you,' Woodrow said instantly. 'Jackson and Townley can guard this place with no trouble. I'll go saddle some horses and bring them here.'

'Make it quick,' Arlen said. 'I've wasted too much time as it is. I need handcuffs.'

Woodrow took two pairs of handcuffs from a bottom drawer of the desk. As he handed them to Arlen someone hammered on the street door. Woodrow sprang up and drew his gun. Arlen dropped the handcuffs and keys on the desk and rested his hand on the butt of his Colt.

'Who is it?' Woodrow called.

'Bill Tobin,' was the answer. 'I've got a message for Marshal Arlen.'

'Who's Tobin?' Arlen queried.

'He works in the big saloon. Shall I open the door?'

'Sure. But don't get between me and the doorway.' Arlen drew his pistol and cocked it.

Woodrow opened the door and stepped aside. A man stood outside, apparently alone and unarmed. He looked at Arlen.

'Are you the marshal?' he demanded.

'I'm Arlen. What's the message and who asked you to pass it on?'

'A man came into the saloon and gave me five dollars to pass on word that Rufus Sandor is on the trail south of town, waiting for you. You're to go alone and unarmed. You got that?'

'Is that all he said?' Arlen demanded.

'He said something about you being aware that he

holds all the aces. If you don't do like he says then Brenda Farrell will be killed.'

Tobin departed. Arlen looked keenly at Woodrow.

'You'd better stay here and watch the place,' he said. 'I'll go alone to hear what Sandor's got to say. He may be trying to draw me away so his gang can come in and bust Frome loose.'

'Don't worry about this place. We'll hold it.'

Arlen nodded. He checked his pistol, then his derringer, and left the office. For a moment he stood on the sidewalk, looking around the street. Then he faced south and set off at a fast walk for the edge of town. The silence surrounding him seemed filled with menace. He kept his mind blank, not wanting to think of what would happen if he lost control of this situation.

He cleared the end of the street and paused. The trail stretched out ahead of him, and he caught his breath when he saw a solitary rider sitting his horse some 300 yards away. He strode forward steadily, his boots creating tiny puffs of dust as he planted them firmly on the trail. Sweat trickled from under his hat brim and ran down his face. He ignored the discomfort. His whole attention was centred on what he had to do.

He saw that the rider was Rufus Sandor long before he reached the spot where the horse was waiting. Sandor had both hands on his reins, and was apparently unarmed. When Arlen was twenty paces from the horse, Sandor called sharply.

'In case you're planning trickery you better know that I have two men covering you with rifles. One is about thirty yards behind you in a dry wash. The other is positioned in

154

the opposite direction. They have orders to shoot you dead if you look like trying anything stupid. And I said for you to come unarmed.'

Arlen halted. His hands were at his sides. 'I'd rather leave my head behind than my pistol. I reckon you've got a hide-out gun on you. So what's the deal?'

'You want Brenda safe with Buck,' Sandor said, 'and I want all the money in the bank and my brother released from the jail. I'll do a straight swap with you. I get what I want and you get the girl back under your protection.'

'I can't do anything about the money,' Arlen said, 'but I can turn Frome loose. Where is Brenda? I want to see that she is unharmed.'

'Look over there to your right.' Sandor lifted his left arm as he spoke and waved it.

Arlen glanced to his right and saw a movement as a man emerged from the cover of some rocks, holding Brenda by an arm. He had a pistol in his hand, the muzzle pointing at Brenda's head.

'I'd like to know what your business is around here,' Arlen said.

'It's none of your business, but I planned to take over the Farrell ranch, and the only way I could get through to Buck was by holding Brenda as a lever against him. Then you came on the scene and spoiled my play.'

'So how do we make the hand-over?' Arlen did not take his gaze off Brenda, and she was watching him. 'I don't trust you an inch, Sandor.'

He caught a sudden movement by Sandor and jerked his attention back to him. Sandor was grinning. His right hand was inside his jacket. Arlen caught a glimpse of a

gun sliding out of the jacket and hurled himself sideways
to the ground, reaching for his pistol as he did so.
Sandor cocked a short-barrelled .38 and swung it to
follow Arlen's movement. Arlen landed on his back on
the hard ground, his gun sweeping up to align the
muzzle on Sandor.

Several guns fired simultaneously. A rifle bullet from
behind Arlen crackled in his right ear as he rolled. He
fired at Sandor a split second before Sandor could cut
loose. Sandor jerked as a slug hit him somewhere in the
body, while his slug bored through the brim of Arlen's
Stetson, jerking it from his head. Arlen saw Sandor's gun
drop to the ground. He swung around, looking for the
rifle that had fired at him, and saw a man standing in a
depression thirty yards away, rifle butt in his shoulder.

Arlen triggered his Colt, aiming high to allow for the
distance. The rifle fired, but the gunman was jerking
under the hammer blow of Arlen's striking slug and his
shot whined over Arlen's head. Arlen looked around for
Brenda. She was struggling with her captor, both hands
on the man's wrist as she tried to take his gun. Arlen
clenched his teeth. He could not get a clear shot at the
gunman.

Hoofbeats hammered on the hard ground and Arlen
threw a glance at Sandor, who was swaying in his saddle
as his horse went at a run along the trail. Arlen lifted his
gun and sent a shot after him, but his mind was on
Brenda and he turned and ran towards her. A second
rifle cut loose at him from the opposite direction and a
slug struck his right thigh in the flesh above the knee. He
went down in a sprawl as his leg gave way; losing his gun

he rolled over on to his back. As he got to his feet he saw the man with Brenda thrust her to the ground and come running towards him.

The man started shooting. Arlen looked around for his Colt. When he failed to see it he reached into his pocket for the derringer. The man came on, firing desperately. Arlen drew a deep breath, took a deliberate aim, and fired. The .41 slug struck the man in the chest and he went down like a sack of chicken meal. Arlen got to his feet and hobbled towards Brenda, who was scrambling to her feet.

Brenda screamed and pointed beyond Arlen. He spun around to see Sandor coming back at him, intent on riding him down. There was blood on Sandor's right shoulder. He was shouting, his mouth wide; his face showing desperation.

Arlen fired the remaining shot in the derringer. The bullet took Sandor in the forehead. Sandor threw up his arms and went sideways out of his saddle. The horse galloped past Arlen and headed for town. Arlen dropped to the ground, his right leg refusing to support him. He looked around for more opposition and spotted a group of horsemen coming out of town. Brenda reached him and dropped to her knees.

'Are you badly hurt?' she demanded.

'It doesn't matter about me. Find my pistol. I dropped it. There are riders coming out of town. They may be Sandor's gang.'

'Forget them,' she said. 'It's the posse coming back. Larrabee's leading them. They obviously didn't go to Beaver Creek.'

Arlen sat up and grasped his thigh with both hands.

The wound did not look as bad as it felt. The bullet had not hit the bone. But it hurt like hell. Larrabee and the posse arrived; the blacksmith looked down at Arlen.

'We didn't go to Beaver Creek,' he said. 'We got close to the Farrell spread and met a cowboy who had passed the creek, and he reported no sign of anyone around there. I reckoned we'd been sent on a wild-goose chase and came back in case Sandor was here. Looks like I was right.'

'Take the posse and look around hereabouts,' Arlen said. 'Pick up any strangers.'

Larrabee rode on with the posse. Arlen removed his neckerchief to tie it around his thigh. It came to him then that the trouble was over, ended by the shot that killed Rufus Sandor. He sighed and looked into Brenda's worried face.

'I reckon your trouble is over,' he told her. 'I guess now I can start back to Dodge City with Frome.'

'You won't be able to ride with a leg wound,' she protested. 'Wire your office that you're hurt, then come out to the ranch and rest up until you've healed.'

'I've got a feeling that if I settled myself out at your place I wouldn't want to leave when the time comes,' he answered, looking into her eyes. 'I've kind of got used to seeing you around.'

'That sounds like a good idea,' she said instantly.

Arlen took a deep breath. 'I wonder if it would work?'

'There's only one way to find out.' Brenda smiled. 'Try it.'

He nodded, and said without hesitation, 'Thanks for the offer. I'll do that. Let's get me to the doc's place, and then I'll send a wire to my office.'

She helped him to his feet and took some of his weight as he limped back into town. Both of them were thinking that it wasn't the end but a new beginning.